COASTAL *Winds*

ADDISON MOTT

Printed in the United States of America
The Young Authors Initiative
Keen Vision Publishing, LLC
www.publishwithkvp.com
ISBN: 978-1-955316-69-9

Everybody has a secret,
You do, and I do too.
They may be good or bad,
but we all have them in common,
no matter our differences.

Table of Contents

Chapter One

THE BEGINNING OF IT ALL

Atlantic Beach, North Carolina, June 2, 2018

I ride my bike across the rocky concrete sidewalk by the beach. The wind blows in my soft, amber hair, kissing it sweetly. The aroma of the coastal winds and salty air fills my lungs. I inhale and exhale with a smile, catching another scent as well. Various flowers sit in the front basket on my bike, and their fragrance tickles my nostrils as I breathe them in gently. I gaze at the ocean and sand, continuing my journey. I stop on my brakes, soon reaching my first destination. I see Galena Edwards, who runs a jewelry stand and is making some seashell earrings. I park my bike and hop off. I walk up to her and admire the collection of seashells she has resting on her stand.

"Hey there, Lon!" She greets, cracking a wrinkly smile.

"Hey," I respond, "I have some seashells for you. I collected them from the beach when we went out, and I thought of you. Here ya go."

I place the shells I pull from my pockets onto the light-beige wood on her stand. Her smile widens, and she holds the shells up and examines them closely. I have known Galena for a time, so I am confident she will love this offering of shells. I am proven right once she turns her attention from the shells back to me.

"Beautiful! Here is something for you," she comments, tossing some money at me.

"Nice, thank you!" I say, catching the money and cracking a smile with wide eyes.

She places the shells on a table filled with thousands of shells, small, big, medium, dark, and light. She turns her head to me, and she beams brightly.

"I thought of you too when I began to make this bracelet," she says as she picks up a beautiful bracelet she picked out for me. She walks towards me, takes my wrist, and slides the bracelet on.

"Perfection." She says as she steps back a bit. I never examine and notice her frisky, frizzy grey afro. It shines in the sunlight that hits her dark yet joyful and blessed face. Her pearly white teeth sparkle as she grins at me. I smile back before I glance at the bracelet on my wrist, in awe of the quality and design. "It's on the house, baby," she adds before she returns to her earrings.

"Why, thank you so much!" I express my appreciation, wanting her to know how much I like the bracelet.

She smiles at me again and says, "When you come back, I'll have something for your parents and siblings."

I nod, my own smile widening at the news. I walk back

over to my bike and wave goodbye, settling on the seat comfortably. Galena waves back at me, and I push off, the wind once more brushing against my face. I do not exactly know where I am going, but I will go wherever God intends for me to go. I glance at my wrist and grin, face bathed in the sunlight. My legs work and pump the pedals of my bike. It does not matter to me how much my legs hurt. I continue to pedal harder and harder with each passing moment—I just want to admire the breeze. I focus back onto the street, and the scent of the salty waters and petite flowers makes me shiver with comfort.

Though, as I look once more at the beach, I am captivated. Most of my attention goes to Carson Blake Wilder. He has his swimwear on as he surfs, weaving through the waves. He is so adorable, and I cannot help but stare like a weirdo, bike continuing straight ahead on the path. His soft tan skin and blond hair make me smile. Though I am not close, I know his bright blue eyes are crinkled and filled with joy and happiness, making me smile even more.

"Watch out!" A raspy voice calls out from in front of me.

Snapping my head forward, I attempt to stop on my brakes, but it is too late. I crash into whomever was unlucky enough to get in my way and fall onto the rough pavement below.

"Ow," I groan, trying to get up.

Whoever they were, they reached out their hand to pull me up. I grab their hand and get up, wiping my eyes. It is my fault the accident happened. Before I can apologize, the person speaks again.

"Watch out next time."

I look at the person I crashed into. He is dark-skinned, with brown curly hair and brown eyes. In addition to his tone of frustration, he looks injured.

"Are you alright? Sorry about crashing into you," I quickly reply, feeling awful.

He cracks a crooked smile and then laughs while I stand there in complete confusion. He stops laughing, collects himself, and asks me, "It was that guy, right?" I slightly tilt my head in more confusion. What is he talking about? Did he hit his head when I crashed into him?

"That made you to crash?" He clarifies, following up on his question.

I shrug, my face flushed, understanding his meaning. Glancing down at my feet, I wince at my red, scraped right knee. I quickly avert my gaze from my knee and look behind me at Carson, who is still surfing. Sighing with relief, I then look back at the stranger who looks around my age.

"Okay, maybe that's true… but are you okay? Did I harm you?" I refocus on the fact I could have hurt him.

He looks at his red elbow and says, "This is nothing new. I have been through worst situations."

I almost ask if he made it a habit to jump in front of moving bikes, but instead, I chuckle and search my pocket for some tissue. I always keep some because Mama says so—even if I do not know why. 'But this is a good circumstance for these,' I think. I get one out and grab his arm, carefully patting his elbow as a bit of blood comes out onto the tissue. He pulls back after a few seconds and thanks me with a warm smile. I smile back before we both turned to pick up our bikes.

"What's your name?" I ask curiously. I had never seen him before. While waiting for an answer, I try to pick up the flowers that had fallen out of my basket and look at him at the same time.

He turns back at me and says plainly, "Nolan."

I smile and introduce myself, "I'm Londyn."

Before the conversation can continue, he suddenly pulls his phone out with a bright, tacky, red case and taps on it.

"I got to go," he mentions, putting his phone back in his pocket.

"Ah, okay," I respond.

He smiles and hops onto his bike. I wave goodbye, and so does he. Once he's gone, I climb back onto my bike and pedal toward the coffee shop. It is just this small shop downtown, close to where I am currently. As I'm riding down the street filled with many small shops, I look around the area, taking in the nostalgic memories and atmosphere it gives. After a few minutes, my mind shifts to something new.

I think back to that boy I crashed into. 'Nolan, was it? Yeah, Nolan,' I remember, picturing him in my mind, bike swaying along the sidewalk. I cannot help but chuckle at his silly tie-dyed shirt and ugly ripped jeans. He really stuck out. Shrugging to myself, I continue to scan my surroundings, not wanting another accident.

That is how I spotted Coraline waving at me from inside the coffee shop's window. My bike comes to a halt, with dust and rocks blasting behind me from my bike. I hop off my bike with excitement and park it. I fling open the door and walk inside, making the shop's bell ring several times.

"You're going to break that door, idiot." Coraline comments, her eyebrows raised so high they could reach the moon but a smile so big it could make the whole state's day.

"No, I'm not!" I argue back with a smile. I put money on the counter, not looking at the menu since I know exactly what I want. "You know what I want," I inform, grinning as she rolls her eyes with a smirk and goes to grab a cup.

I look behind me and into the blue sky, thinking about what I might do today. I feel all eyes on me, but I do not mind. While I'm waiting, I open my phone and scroll through various apps. A few minutes pass, and I hear a thud on the counter.

"Enjoy, Lon," Coraline announces.

I look in front of me and see my coffee sitting there.

"Thank you!" I say with pleasure and a soft smile as I pick up my drink. I then take a sip, voicing my approval once more. "It's amazing! Thank you again!"

"What are your parents going to say about you drinking this much caffeine?" Coraline questions. I look down at my shoes, having no answer. "Aha!" She hollers a split second later, obviously knowing I'd be in some trouble.

With Coraline, I'm not worried about her ratting me out. She smiles at me and leans on the counter. Before she can tease me any further, one of her coworkers yells at her. Since she is thoroughly distracted, I walk out and sit outside on one of the chairs with a small table, snickering at the incident. Coraline is sixteen with a huge personality and sarcastic humor. I like her because you can never go wrong with a great friend like her—even when I can see her getting scolded at work.

Shaking my head, I sip my coffee until nothing is left to sip but air. I put down my drink and watch the cars pass by for a bit since I'm in no big hurry. Eventually, I get up from my seat, go to the garbage, and throw away my empty cup. I peer through the window of the coffee shop and see Coraline arguing with one of the employees while trying to mix up an order. I chuckle to myself as I watch her animated gestures. Since I would be back another day, I didn't need to go in and say my goodbyes.

I hop on my bike, kick the stand behind me, and pedal off. I inhale the gas fumes and salty air, filling up my lungs. I then exhale, and I cannot help but smile as I feel lighter than before. Cruising down the street, small shops and fast cars pass all around me with the soft blue sky as their backdrop. The sun shines proudly high upon me, making me strain my eyes. Pedaling harder and faster, I again come across the beach area, safely gliding along the sidewalk. I smile at the sight of the salty water and sand, knowing many have traced these places with their footsteps.

I feel nostalgic as I take in the scenery and the smells. Every smell takes me to a different moment. I can smell my own scent, too; I smell like a farm, and the very scent transports me to yesterday when my family and I went to that farm with goats and horses. The scent clinging to my lips, past the coffee, reminds me of the hours spent at home this morning. It causes me to recall how my stomach was full of a chocolate chip Frappuccino and a tasty chocolate-filled cookie I had eaten before leaving home. Soon, I would be home.

I take the sharp turn that follows a road leading towards my house. Houses lined up, side by side, meet my eyes. The freshly cut grass from our neighbors who worship their lawn makes me glance at their yard. I look at the red birds that hover above me and sit in a tree. Even though these are sights I see every day, they still draw my attention. So much so that I did not notice the large rock sitting menacingly on the sidewalk. I soon found myself crashing for the second time today.

My face plants itself into the rough pavement, creating scratches and an uncomfortable feeling. My body aches and tinges, announcing the pain that will linger for the rest of the day. Overhead, I hear Nolan's rough, raspy voice, a voice becoming familiar to me.

"Second time today?"

"Yeah," I bemoan as I try to collect myself. I lift my

head to see him reaching out his hand. I weakly lift my arm up and let him grab on as he tries to pull me up. I glance towards my house. "Thanks," I mumble, wincing.

"Do you get distracted easily?" He says as he looks where I was.

"I guess," I admit, bending down to pick up my phone, which, thank the Lord, does not have any cracks.

"You guess?" He says with a smirk. I just nod with embarrassment. "You look like you got into a fight with a feisty cat!" He adds with a chuckle.

"You should not be talking," I say, chuckles blending in with his. "And is everything funny to you?" I say as I collect myself.

He snarks jokingly, "Yeah, when it comes to you."

I look at him with a smile, asking, "Me, specifically?"

"No, silly, I'm not a loner," he retorts with a laugh.

"Yeah, okay…" I say, rolling my eyes, still chuckling. I look behind him and see my house, remembering my destination. "Hey, I have to go home. I'll see you around," I inform him as I quickly collect my things and mount my bike.

"Run off, I guess." He says with a sarcastic tone.

I smile and wave at him as I pedal off. I notice his eyes are still locked onto me right before he runs off. This time, I make sure I watch the path in front of me as I ride into the yard. Soon, I park my bike in the garage of my home, and I hop off, taking the delicate flowers into my hands. I walk over to the button that closes the garage door. Every ache of the day calls for my attention, so I search for the first aid kit once I put the flowers down. It is a slow process since my body protests each movement, but I easily find the first aid kit and get to work.

As I apply some bandages to my scratches and scrapes, I realize that my parents are not home because their car was not in the garage when I arrived. Instead, the babysitter's car was in the garage. Putting the first aid kit away and picking up the flowers, I curiously open the door that leads to the laundry room from the garage, and I walk into the hallway to the living room, figuring someone would be there. I am proven right when someone pops up from their seated position on the couch.

"What happened to you?" Avery immediately asks, concern lacing her voice.

Avery is my eldest sister; we are three years apart. Ethan, my brother, comes rushing out of his room. Ethan is one year older than me and is obsessed with video games and gamer YouTubers. I find the things he likes to be cringy, but it is whatever. The babysitter, Ms. Fredrick, comes out from the kitchen, having heard the commotion. Despite the newcomers, I recall Avery's question since she's still looking at me with a critical eye.

"It's nothing. I kept falling off my bike," I reassure Avery, brushing some dirt and dust from my clothes.

Before anyone asks more questions, I take the flowers and put them in the vase with a couple more on the coffee table. While I admire my arrangement, Ms. Fredrick signals me to the bathroom to take a shower. I look forward to a shower, knowing it will soothe some of my aches. So, I hastily excuse myself and make my way out of the living room. Once in my room, I choose some clothes to wear for when I am done showering before I head to the bathroom. Hopping in the shower, my mind flashes to the events of the day.

Specifically, I think of the new person I met, Nolan. Shaking my head at the embarrassing times in my day, I cannot but feel stupid, as if I took a "cringy and clumsy girl" dynamic. I grimace and shake my head again, trying to chase away those thoughts. The sound of the water against the tiles helps me clear my mind a little—though soon, my phone buzzes from a notification. I want to peek but cannot since I'm in the middle of getting cleaned up, which makes me frustrated. I speed up my process, feeling a little re-energized!

Once I'm done, I hop out of the shower and change into fresh clothes. Steam escaped from the shower. So many scents swirling around me. I smell the fresh and clean fragrance of the clothes I have on—and I especially smell the scent of my body wash and shampoo. I inhale and exhale with a smile. I leave the bathroom with my hair still dripping a little and head into my bedroom. I hear Ethan and Avery argue like always, but I ignore it and flop onto my bed, phone clutched in my hand.

I sigh as I check my phone since it was a useless notification about the weather. Shifting on my bed, I decide I should call Hailee, who has been my best friend since elementary school. We grew up together like sisters since we first met in church through our mamas, who both knew each other from high school. Putting the phone up to my ear, I dial Hailee's number.

"Hey, Hailee!" I greet her excitedly once she picks up.

"Hey, Lon. What are you up to?" Hailee responds.

"Nothing, I just got out of the shower," I say.

"Oh, I was just about to get in the shower!" She tells me, chuckling.

We both laugh as I reply, "Okay, I'll let you get in the shower."

"Bye!"

She hangs up afterward. 'That was quick,' I think to myself. With nothing to do, a thought pops into my mind. I have not drawn anything in a while, so I close my phone, reach over to the drawer, and open it, revealing my notebook. Grabbing the notebook and opening it up, I glance through the pages until I find an empty page. Soon, I let my imagination take over. I think of this girl with black hair and hazel eyes. I do not know where the image comes from. I just follow whatever comes to my mind.

As I draw, I can hear a commotion in the other room as Avery and Ethan playfight and argue. I chuckle to myself and continue to sketch away, the once-empty page coming to life with my creation.

Chapter Two

LIGHTS, CAMERA, AND A SMALL CRUSH

Atlantic Beach, North Carolina, June 6, 2018

It is around 11:40 in the morning when I hear Mama call for my brother, Ethan. I rub my eyes and groan, flipping to the other side of the bed. The bed sheets are so warm that I want to drown in them. My eyes feel heavy, and I fall asleep in seconds. Though, I do not get to sleep for long. The next thing I know, Mama is knocking on my door, jolting me from my slumber.

"Lon, you must get up. We are going somewhere," Mama calls.

I open my puffy eyes to the light from my curtains glistening and shining light into my room, making my beige walls stand out and wood flooring shine. I do not want to get up, but I know Mama isn't going to go away. In fact, I soon hear Mama open my door and walk into my room, so I turn over towards her. She sits on my bed beside me and caresses my hair with her soft, slim fingers.

"The day needs you," Mama says with a soft tone.

I look at her and cannot help but think about how beautiful she is. She pats my shoulder and signals me to get up, breaking me from my thoughts. Without complaint, I get up from bed, rubbing my eyes, and Mama starts to walk out of my room. She sticks her head out before closing the door all the way.

"Get changed, alright?"

I nod, and she smiles at me before shutting the door. I go into my closet, pick an outfit, and change my clothes. Once done, I head into the bathroom and brush my teeth, able to hear Mama and Ethan arguing. I spit out the toothpaste and rinse my mouth. I love the taste and feel of a clean mouth. Afterward, I wash my face, brush my hair, apply Chapstick, and am ready…

"Londyn!" My Mama calls.

I rush out of the bathroom and see my squad.

"We decided that instead of spending the day wasting our energy on our electronics, we can go see a movie," Mama announces.

Well, that is clearly not a unanimous decision. I already see Ethan on his phone. Mama nudges him and signals him to change. Ethan saunters to the bedroom before going into the bathroom.

"I'll go ahead and start the car up," Papa informs us.

Mama nods at Papa's comment. They both head into the garage. The silence that follows their exit feels eerie. It is quiet. Really quiet. I decide to break the silence, turning to my sister, Avery.

"Since they went to the car, why couldn't we?" I say as I open the garage door and hear Papa and Mama squabbling in the white Honda. Once they see us, they stop abruptly.

"Okay..." Avery speaks hesitantly.

We get into the car and hear Ethan's loud footsteps stomping as he advances towards the garage. He opens the door to the garage, closes it behind him, and then hops into the car.

"Are we late?" Ethan questions.

"Plenty of time," says Papa, a smile curling.

Papa has a soft smile on his face, while Mama has an unusual frown. It is extremely rare to see her in this state. Papa begins to drive, pulling out of the garage, and then rolls down our windows. I am sitting in the middle, Ethan on my right and Avery on my left. Papa tries to roll down Mama's window, but she refuses by exposing her hand and shaking her head. Avery and I notice, but it is Avery who speaks.

"Are you alright, Ma'?"

Mama turns to us with a smile. Her smile is a fib, and her "Yes" answer is also a fib. I do not know how to process it, so I turn my attention to other things, my wallet clutched in my hands. My eyes stray over to Avery. I never noticed how similar my hair color is to Avery's. Everyone talks about it, but I never agree with them. Her fair, thin hair flows in the wind like fish's fins do as they swim. Her hazel eyes sparkle in the sunlight, while mine just stay solid all the time. I am interrupted from my musing by

Ethan's movements beside me. Ethan puts in his earbuds and looks out the window, but that doesn't last long as he soon takes one earbud out and grimaces at Avery.

"Oh, my great heavens, can't you stop pretending you're in some movie?" He complains.

"I'm sorry that I just want to have a grand time!" Avery exclaims bitterly.

"Stop it!" Papa roars. "Now, just stop this arguing! We decided to go to the movies, and we will have a great time as a family!"

After Papa's outburst, it is silent as a mouse. Soon, Ethan scoffs, interrupting the silence. But the tension still lingers and is awkward. I look out the window to see passing cars, buildings, a brilliant blue sky, and… Nolan? Nolan is on his bike, going in the opposite direction from where our vehicle is going. My mind transitions to the movies as I remember where we are headed.

I am excited to go to the movies since we have not gone there in a while! It is a bit early—at least to me—but it can create a closer bond. I was still worried about Mama, though, my eyes straying to her. She is just looking out the window of the car, silent. I ponder on what my parents were talking about back in the garage that made it so heated. Again, the thoughts are too much to consider, so I let my mind drift to random things for the rest of the ride. Soon enough, we arrive at our destination, Papa parking the car.

"Alright, y'all, let's head inside. Stick beside your Mama and Pops, you hear?" Papa exclaims.

Everyone nods, getting out of the car. There it is, the Atlantic Station Cinema. Again, I have not seen this movie theater in years, and it feels nostalgic. I wish I could feel that feeling again when I came here for the first time. It was incredible. Walking forward, my hair blows in my face by the gust of wind that rushes over us. I get the chills, but I never regret living at the beach. I love it—it smells nice, and it smells like me. It feels like home.

We make our way inside, and I remember this place all too well—the silly patterned flooring me and Ethan always mocked and that unforgettable red booth. This place is always clean, and the employees are incredibly nice. I know what my favorite part of the cinema is, though. It was never the movies—instead, it was picking out the candy. In fact, I loved picking out our candy! Mama always told us, "Not too much, but not too less."

As we wait in line, feeling like a billion years have passed until it is close to our turn, I look around and freeze… Who is that? Is that Carson and his new girlfriend? I was not expecting to see them. My heart pounds in my chest—only the feeling grows worse as I turn and see, behind a group of people, Courtney! No way is she going to see me like this. No way is she going to see me with my embarrassing siblings. Of all the people to see, it had to be Courtney Gracelyn, the girl who humiliated me in front of the whole lunchroom in 3rd grade. I still have not forgiven her for that. She always thinks she is better than someone else. This hatred is not so great overall. I did not realize how deep in thought I was because, before

I noticed, we are already close to the booth.

Mama starts to speak and tell us the same thing, "Not too much, but-"

"Not too less, Mama!" Ethan finishes her sentence.

Mama gives a brilliant smile and pats Ethan's shoulder to signal for him, Avery, and me to pick out our items. We all rush to get what we all want, and of course, we all pick similar candies.

"Stop being copycats!" Ethan comments.

"We are not!" I respond.

"Are too!" Ethan says, sticking his tongue out.

"Says the one who—"

My sentence is soon adjourned by Papa, who interrupts the fun, though he is normally the one who "invented fun." He waves to us with our tickets impatiently. We walk towards our parents with a sort of dread. I am worried because Papa ruined our fun, and things will not be so fun anymore. I try not to think this because Mama and Papa said to live our lives to the fullest without dread, sorrow, or worry. So, I try to do this by thinking of something more joyful. I try to think about that new movie we are going to watch. I saw it in a lot of advertisements on social media. It will surely be a fun movie, and I cannot help but think about it.

Mama and Papa carry the candy and the popcorn while my siblings and I carry the drinks. The drinks were cold and made my hands freeze. The smell of coke, Doritos, cherry-flavored sweets, and yes… the popcorn. The buttery popcorn that I always try to catch in my mouth and melts on my tongue. The popcorn reminds me of the summer two years ago on my birthday when I tried to catch it in my mouth, and my siblings soon joined in. The summer when we tried to hit the piñata, blindfolded. I chuckle to myself. I almost hit Avery that day, and her reaction was worth every moment! I snap back to reality when I hear Avery snap at me.

"Were you dreaming of Carson?" she asks, smiling and raising her eyebrows.

"No, just that time I almost hit you with that bat," I tease and chuckle, barely keeping myself from laughing aloud.

"Shut up," she says, nudging me and causing me to almost drop the drinks.

"Behave," Papa warns, ruining the fun yet again.

I try to explain, "We were just—"

"I do not want to hear it." Papa firmly states, cutting me off.

What? This was not like Papa at all. I did not get it. Why is he acting like this now? No one says anything, so I keep quiet as well. Soon enough, we're entering the theater, and it at once gets dark with only the bright light of the large screen. I am so excited and can ignore Papa's words and strange attitude. Advertisements are playing on the screen, specifically car ads, but we pay no mind as we follow Mama up the steps to our seats. We put down our belongings and finally put the cold drinks into the cup holders. I try to rub the freezing condensation from the drinks off my hands. Mama sees my struggle and gives me a napkin to dry it off, so I thank her with a grateful smile.

The screen signals us to turn our phones off. The movie is about to start, and I always love the excitement I feel beforehand. The lights are going off, and my heart is racing. I smile while my siblings relax in their chairs. Sure, it might seem immature to them, but it is perfectly normal to me. I watch the movie with anticipation and joy—and once the movie is over, I cannot help but feel pumped and ready to take on the world! Ethan is childishly jumping around, acting like one of the characters from the film. I am beyond embarrassed...

"Stop! You're embarrassing me," I mutter, covering my face and looking down.

"Whatever." He responds as he stops to pick at and bother me.

Ignoring him, I am glad I thought ahead and kept some of the cotton candy for myself. Papa opens the doors as we walk out, and the wind starts teasing and blowing in my hair. I attempt to get it out of my face because it is bugging me—though not as much as Ethan. I hit him with my bag of cotton candy.

"Stop!" I demand.

"Shut up," He dictates, not taking me seriously.

I roll my eyes, open the car door, and hop inside. I open my phone as I hear my annoying brother and Papa mimic the characters in the movie. With their similar brunette hair, it's like watching a big version and a mini version of the same person.

"I'm just trying to have fun, kids. Are you guys too old?" Papa retorts.

"No," I say, punching in my password on my phone.

"Okay, well, you're not old enough to jam out to this," Papa jokes as he turns on the radio to my favorite song, Bad Reputation by Joan Jett & The Blackhearts.

Mama carves a smile for me, twists around in her seat, and puts her two hands out in front of me for me to reach out to. I take her hands and smile as we jammed out to the song. Avery puts her elbow on my shoulder and joins our horrid singing. Papa starts the car and backs out of the parking lot, grinning to himself. Ethan frowns, rolls his eyes, and fumbles with his change. Ethan always thinks he is too smart, funny, or superior to something, which makes me sing even louder. Avery takes the bait and raises her voice to match with me. Ethan groans and does his best to ignore us.

As we're rolling down the road, heading back home, I notice something: Mama's smile is not fake anymore. It is real. I am glad Mama is back, even if it is temporary. I smile even larger and jam out with her as she swings her beautiful, dirty blonde hair. I am glad it is medium-length and does not hit Papa in the face. That thought makes me laugh, adding to my joy. Speaking about Papa, he glances over at Mama. He looks at Mama with an expression. An expression I cannot put into words. My song becomes an advertisement as Mama tries to catch her breath and Avery clears her throat.

Ethan scoffs, "Goodness, Avery, your vocals sound

like a cat dying!"

I chuckle, and Avery smiles and shrugs. Ethan flicks his head, and I murmur a small "ouch" in response.

"That goes for you too. Take some lessons from me," Ethan says haughtily.

I then flick his head and ask as a comeback, "What lessons?"

The comment starts a chain reaction in the car. Avery starts to snort, and I laugh with her. I hear Mama snicker, too. Papa follows along, and eventually, so does Ethan.

"Stop, you guys. You're going to make me crash!" Papa says, wiping tears from his eyes from the aftermath of laughing hard.

"Well, we don't want that!" Avery exclaims, following more laughter from us.

The car ride remains upbeat. So much so that before I knew it, we were already riding our neighborhood streets. I glance at Nolan's house and see him helping his grandma with decorations. Ah! That is the reason I had never seen him before. It should have been so clear; he is new here. So, I believe he might go into 8th grade with me. Something about this idea makes me long for 8th grade now. Soon enough, he's out of sight as we turn into our yard. The garage door opens, and Papa drives inside to the park. We all get out, close our doors, and walk inside the house. I place my candies on the counter for a brief second, but I then spy Ethan, who glances at my candy, so I quickly snatch it off and go to my room.

Once inside my bedroom, I change out of my dirty

clothes and into something more comfortable: a blue shirt with my favorite artist on the front and knee-length blue jean shorts. I put everything away, jump onto my bed, and open my candy to relax and scroll on social media. I giggle at silly videos of animals being mindless. I hear bags being put down elsewhere and talking in the kitchen. I cannot hear what they are saying, but it is annoying, distracting me from my relaxation. I put in my earbuds, turn on some music, and then move to open the drawer and grab my notebook. I am not the best artist in the world, but I enjoy it as a hobby. I grab a 2B pencil and got to work. I am always so focused on my work. I ignore the world around me and focus on one thing: drawing. I sometimes forget the music is on. I sometimes forget that everything exists.

I do not know how long I have been drawing, but after some time, I decide to peer out my window, and I see Nolan kicking some rocks and getting his phone out. I watch for a bit before I get back to drawing and allow it to consume me again. I start to think. I am always thinking. I do not know what I want to be when I grow up. When I was younger, I wanted to be a teacher. I admired the teachers, including Mrs. Robinson. She was sweet like honey. I loved how she would be so kind to the kids even though they were terrible. I wish I were as patient as her. But these days, I do not want to be a teacher anymore. I wish I knew what I wanted to be…

I hear a loud knock at the front door over my music, bringing me out of my thoughts. I pop out my earbuds and hear Mama greeting someone at the door. I get up and drop my supplies on my bed. I walk on the cold wood floor and glide to my bedroom door to hear better. Even through the door, I can hear Nolan smile through his words. His raspy voice is so recognizable to me now. I then hear Papa, "Is there anything we can do for you, like move furniture or paint walls?"

I open my bedroom door, deciding it is time to leave. I did not want it to seem like I was trying to hide away. I head for the front of the house, where all the commotion is taking place. As I emerge from the hallway, I see an older lady, who I assume to be Nolan's grandma, standing with Nolan, and I smile awkwardly. They stand outside on the stoop, but my parents soon invite them inside.

Once inside, Nolan gives me a small wave, and I wave back. I did not want to give a bad first impression to his grandma. I follow everyone to the living room with those sage green walls. In the living room, Ethan is already sitting by the fireplace on the chair, so I sit by Papa, Mama, and Avery on the couch. Nolan and his grandma sit on the grey sofa across from the couch. It is quiet for a second until the woman assumed to be Nolan's grandma, introduced as Ms. Price, breaks it.

"We moved here since we had heard it was a thriving state," Ms. Price explains.

"Yes, we heard that too. Our house wasn't much of a home, so we found some land here and moved," Papa responds, nodding.

"We heard there was a fantastic education system and

schools here, too," Ms. Price comments further, putting her arm around Nolan and looking at him sweetly. Nolan looks as if he could not be any more embarrassed. He gives a straight smile, showing his teeth and expressing his faze. He tries to get from under Ms. Price's arm, managing to do so after a few seconds of subtle struggle. Ms. Price continues as if he didn't move, stating, "We haven't gotten him in school since it is summer break."

"Yeah, these kiddos have got to go back to school before they drive us insane!" Papa says, smirking.

The parents laugh, not caring that none of us kids laugh with them. We all kind of smile to present the idea that we were smiling and giggling along—when we really were not. It feels like years of hearing them gab. I rest my head on my fist, waiting for this to end. To pass the time, I look at the grey couch, the sage walls, the fireplace made of stone, the wooden flooring, then the clock, and Nolan. Shifting in my seat, I watch Mama get up and go into the kitchen to get some cookies she had baked, as I could smell them from the kitchen. There is awkward tension in the air, and the smell of freshly baked cookies makes my stomach growl a bit. I try to cover my stomach from the noise as Mama returns, handing a box to Ms. Price.

"Thank you," Ms. Price says.

Mama moves to sit back down, nodding her head and accepting the thanks. I sit back, sinking into the cushions, as Mama settles into her spot.

"Well, considering how you guys have probably been around the block and discovering the town, has Nolan bumped into any of my kiddos before?" Mama asks.

I almost laugh, thinking, 'Tell me about it. Bumped into? Yeah! Around two times!' I stay quiet, though, wondering if Nolan mentioned those times to his grandma. Ms. Price smiles and nods, making me curious.

"Ah yes, Nolan told me something about meeting a girl," Ms. Price answers. I nod and smile, looking at Nolan—only to notice he is looking at me, too. Ms. Price isn't done speaking, though. Soon, as she grabs her keys, she says, "Alrighty… I think we are going to take our leave."

"Glad to have you in the neighborhood!" Mama exclaims, getting up from her seat and hugging Ms. Price.

Papa also gets up and disappears briefly, and the rest of us get up from our seats. We all head toward the front door, walking the duo out. Before they leave, though, Papa catches up to them to say one last thing.

"Hey, and if you need anything again, call us."

Papa had apparently left to write down two phone numbers on a piece of paper from his local notepad on the coffee table. He hands the paper to Ms. Price, who nods and thanks him before she and Nolan leave. Mama waves after them before she shuts the door.

With company gone, Papa places his notebook on the coffee table, sits on the couch, and turns on the TV. Mama and my siblings go into the kitchen to clean up. I know Ethan would not do anything but sit on the bar stool and scroll on his phone. He is just like Papa. Since everyone else is occupied, I go into my bedroom and grab my phone. I open it to check the time. It is around 3:50 P.M. I start to consider the rest of my day, but I soon hear a knock at the front door again. Curious, I leave my room to check who it is—and to my surprise, it is Nolan. I open the door and raise one brow to see him smiling.

"I asked Grandma if it was all right, and she said so. Do you want to go to the beach? I have never seen it," Nolan tells me, glancing at the beach with bushes trying to cover its beauty.

I nod, smiling, and respond, "I am going to ask Ma' and Papa, but I know they will not mind. It is summer anyway, right?" I hold up a finger, informing him to wait before I leave him on the doorstep, and rush towards the space between the living room and kitchen. "Hey, can I go to the beach with Nolan?" I ask.

Papa is already suspicious, raising an eyebrow and crossing his arms. Mama does the same. I only blink in response, waiting for their answer.

"With that boy?" Papa asks, glancing at the door where Nolan stands patiently.

I nod, and to my relief, Mama nods, too.

"As long as you are safe, girl," she says, wiping the counters.

I wait for Papa's response.

"Do not do anything stupid," Papa starts. "I love you. Yes, you can go," he finishes, tilting his head to the door. I say a quick thanks to him as I rush towards the door to inform Nolan of their decision.

"I think they find us suspicious, but it's okay," I tell

Nolan. "Be right back!"

Once again, leaving Nolan on the doorstep, I hurry back to my room, grab my phone, put it in my back pocket, and look around to see what else I could bring. Nothing comes to mind, so I leave my room.

"Okay, I am going with Nolan now!"

Mama peeked from the corner and told us to be safe. I nod and put on my shoes before I step out of the house. We begin our trek to the beach, Nolan falling into step beside me. Almost immediately, the wind hits me, and my hair blows in my face, so I hurriedly pull it into a ponytail. Nolan smiles at me, making look over at him curiously.

"Your hair looks good up," he comments.

"Sure," I reply, rolling my eyes.

"No, I'm serious!" He insists.

I chuckle at his statement, deciding to let the compliment sit. We walk on the hot concrete while the sun beats down on our sun-kissed skin. I look down at my dirty white shoes, trying to think of a conversation to have, but Nolan beats me to it.

"Can I tell you something crazy?" he asks, and my head automatically lifts to look at him.

"Go ahead," I tell him, wondering what he wants to say.

"I actually have a hard time making friends," he reveals, and my mouth drops.

"But you are such a fun person!" I shout, recalling our few interactions thus far.

He chuckles as his head drops, saying, "I have not

really met anyone else here except for you and your sibling, kind of."

"You're the only kid I've really spent my summer with outside of my house, besides my siblings and Hailee," I say, nodding.

"Who is Hailee?" He questions.

"My best friend," I answer. I am not good at continuing conversations, but I awkwardly shift the topic to something I am curious about. "Speaking of siblings and whatnot, do you have any?"

"Yeah, I do," he answers as he looks at the sky, thinking and squinting his eyes. "I have one, and he is in college." I smile at his answer.

"Does it get lonely?" I follow up, unable to imagine life without Avery and Ethan in the house.

"Yeah, it sure does. He was a good older brother and role model," Nolan says, his tone hinting at something I can't decipher.

I smile in sympathy at his response. I want to ask about his parents, but something tells me I should not. I consider it a gut feeling. Everything about him makes me a little curious, but I've been told I am too nosey for my own good sometimes. Sighing, I look around and notice we have arrived at the beach.

"We're here!" I announce, spreading my arms out.

"We sure are," he replies, smiling and looking around.

"Where did you come from, like what state?" I say in curiosity, wanting to keep the conversation flowing.

"Colorado." He responds.

"That's far!" I say in disbelief.

"Sure is." He speaks.

"I have a favorite spot here on the beach, you know," I inform him, taking off my shoes and watching as he follows my lead and takes his off.

"Ah!" He yelps, jumping up and down.

"What?" I say, shocked and confused.

"This wood, it's so hot!" He says, running into the sand and making me chase after him.

"Well, the sand's hotter!" I holler at him as he runs towards the ocean.

I glance over at Galena, and she smiles at me, nodding. Focusing in front of me again, I finally catch up with Nolan when he reaches the ocean waves. He sits down, and so do I. My eyes scan him, looking him over. He is stunning. I want to say he looks more majestic than Carson. His brown eyes become gold, and his brown hair shines like the sun. He looks over at me, making my heart flutter like a butterfly flying in there.

"Um," I am at a loss for words, quivering under his gaze before a conversation starter jumps out. "What are your hobbies?"

"I love to draw." He says, making me gasp and almost jump up.

"Me too!" I reply, smiling as my response clearly makes him happy.

"What's your favorite color?" He questions.

"Navy blue. It's so underrated," I comment.

He nods his head in agreement before responding, "It

sure is... Are you a dog or cat person?"

I look at the brilliant, outstanding blue sky, asking for answers. I do not have a pet currently, so I am not sure how to answer at first.

"I don't know, maybe cat person," I finally admit.

He shrugs and tilts his head, commenting, "I was always a dog person." He did look like a dog person.

"I understand where you're coming from," I say, chuckling.

"Thank you." He comments out of the blue.

"For what exactly?" I say, confused by the gratitude shown.

"For being here and just," he starts before looking at the glimmering water and back at me, staring into my eyes that mirror the ocean. "Being here with me and—can I say it?" he questions me.

"What?" I respond.

"Being my friend. Thank you, Londyn." He finishes.

I smile and look into his eyes that glistened like honey, saying, "You're welcome. I'm glad to have met you." I look away from him and look behind me, feeling someone's gaze—only to see Galena with her cheek resting on her fist, looking at us sweetly. Did she think we were together or something? I smile, hoping so. I turn back to Nolan, who is looking at the ocean. "Do you want some hand-made beach jewelry?" I question.

Nolan looks curious at my words, so I stand up, brushing the sand from my body. I hold out my hand for him to take, and after a few seconds of consideration, he takes up. I watch him get up and brush the sand off himself before leading him to the stand. I do not know what the rest of the summer has in store, but I feel immensely glad I bumped into Nolan four days ago. What I thought would be nothing but embarrassment has turned into a friendship.

Chapter Three

A BITTER PILL I SWALLOW

Atlantic Beach, North Carolina, June 18, 2018

It is 9:13 am, and I dread waking up so early during the summer. The sun is beaming down on me, warming my skin. Since Mama and Papa are going out to lunch, a babysitter will watch over us today. I want to roll over and go back to sleep, but as I hear a creak from the door as more light shines in from the living room, I know that is out of the question.

"Wake up," whispers Mama as she hovers over me, adding, "It's time to get up. You have a full day ahead of you."

I try to fake sleep, hoping she would not notice I was already awake. She does notice as she chuckles softly and shakes me with excitement. I hear Papa from the dining room handing out breakfast and yelling, "Get up," throughout the house. I give up my act at the call and flop on my side. The warm sheets tempt me, but Mama uncovers me, and I finally open my eyes. She smiles ever so warmly, making me want to smile back and get up like she asked.

So, I rub my eyes to adjust to the lighting, absently picking out the crust from my eyes and getting up. It takes some time for me to stop swaying in my spot, but eventually, I am ready to join the rest of the world—or at least my family. Yawning, I stumble out of my bedroom and head for the dining room with my sloppy pajamas dragging on the cold tiles. When I arrive, Ethan is on his phone, and Avery is talking to Papa. They all stop and look at me, and I can only blink sleepily and give a weak wave.

"Finally, somebody woke up," Ethan snarks, laughing.

Papa nudges him on the side and pulls out my chair, inviting me to sit. I sit down, soon yawning again. While I wait for everyone to get their plates together, I think about the last time I saw Nolan. I have been waiting for Nolan to come back from his aunt's. I never got his number, so I cannot exactly communicate with him. With a sigh, I shake my head and look over my plate, ensuring I have everything I want. Once everyone else is ready and seated, we then pray and dig in. As we eat our pancakes with eggs, Mama and Papa discuss where they will have lunch while Ethan and Avery fight over the last piece of bacon as I sit examining in amusement.

"Cut it out!" Papa hollers.

Ethan and Avery adjust before I break out into a laugh. The rest of breakfast flies by, and soon Mama is collecting the dishes and scolding Ethan to do his turn to clean the dishes. Avery leaves the dining room to clean her room while I take out the trash. The sun shines proudly and confidently in the sky as it shines upon me. I can hear the scraping against the concrete as I dreadfully drag the trash bag behind me. I throw the trash in the garbage bin, but before I can open the door to go back inside, I hear something from afar...

"Londyn!"

The voice sounds oddly familiar. Again, I recall Nolan leaving for his aunt's, but he never did tell me when he was coming back. As I turn, I cannot help but smile as I watch him run up towards me.

"Nolan?"

He looks behind him as his grandma calls out to him. She waves at me, so I wave back with an awkward smile. I still don't know her very well, and I want to make sure she has a good impression of me. Thankfully, Nolan, who stands in front of me, steals my attention.

"Would you like to go to the beach? I miss it..." He says with a sigh.

"I would, but Mama and Papa are going away to eat lunch today," I explain, glancing behind me.

"Oh, okay," He responds with a frown before he asks, "Can't I spend some time here then?"

I see nothing wrong with that, so I shrug, move to the door, and open it to holler for my parents' permission. Papa says, "Sure!" as he puts on his tie in the kitchen. I shut the door and walk back to Nolan.

"What'd he day?" He ponders.

"He said yes," I say, grabbing his hand to head inside. I hear his grandma holler from their vintage maroon truck.

"I got to go help my granny unpack," Nolan interprets.

I frown and sigh, commenting, "Alrighty..." I chuckle and sarcastically add, "Run off, I guess..."

"Don't take my line!" He yells at me as he runs towards his grandma to help her.

I shake my head and go inside. I am only a few feet inside when Papa catches my eyes in his bedroom. I move to thank him for letting Nolan come over, but Papa puts a thick book in a drawer as fast as lightning. He acts like I caught him doing something bad, sparking my interest, and my eyes narrow.

"Papa," I say with suspicion, "what was that?"

"Nothing dear, just... something." He murmurs.

I am not the only one watching him, either. Mama looks at him with a glance of suspicion and qualm. I have never seen Papa act so secretive—unless it was about presents for our birthdays or Christmas. I am overthinking about all this, though. It is now 10:59 am, and I simply stand there thinking about how different Papa had been acting. I feel a little silly, so I head for my room, go inside, and open my phone. I see notifications about the weather, Snapchat, Netflix, and someone else's story. I am uninterested in any of it, so I close my phone and plummet onto my bed, thinking I would take a short nap.

Unfortunately, I then hear arguing. As I listen, I realize

it is not Ethan and Mama, Avery and Papa, or Ethan and Avery, but instead, it is Mama and Papa. I frown, getting up from my bed and hearing someone knocking at my door. I open the door, worried about what or who I might find.

"Mama and Papa's fighting again."

Standing there is Avery with a worried look. She announces their fighting as if the whole house cannot hear them. I do not snark, though, because I am also unsettled.

"I remember," I say, thinking back to them arguing in the car.

"No, it's not that," she says, trying to come inside. Ethan, who I did not initially notice, follows. I let them in and shut my door.

"What do you mean by it's not like that?" I question, wondering if she even knew what I was talking about.

"They argued last night, and I heard something slam on the floor. I—" Avery holds back tears, continuing, "I don't know if it was Mama he threw or some heavy object."

"If it were to be Mama, then we would see a nasty bruise or bump," Ethan speaks before silence could follow.

I nod at Ethan's words, trying to erase my frown. Mama and Papa have been acting off for a bit now—not just together but individually. My mind goes back to the earlier incident with Papa and that book. What was he hiding?

"When did they start to argue like this?" I say wistfully.

Avery fiddles with her sleeve, and Ethan looks around

my room and back at Avery, expecting her to speak. Avery looks at me with tears in her eyes. I blink, curious, tilting my head. What's going on?

"They always argued." I am confused by Avery's words, shaking my head and thinking she is mistaken. She nods and weakly maintains, "I was so young, and they would scream. I never thought much of it since my dolls just distracted me. They had already had Ethan, and I was the one who took care of him!"

Before I can process her words, Avery breaks down in front of us. She cries and crumbles to the floor. I am shocked, turning to Ethan, hoping he understands what's happening. Ethan is watching her. For the first time, I see him about to cry. He always said he was too tough to cry, so that is how I know things are really not okay.

"They blame me!" Avery weeps.

Ethan pats her shoulder and mumbles, "Me too," as he moves to the floor beside Avery. I join them on the floor, though I think it is also because my legs have lost strength as I take in the scene before me. It shatters my heart to see her cry like that. In the background, my parents' arguing is the soundtrack. I attempt to focus and listen to their argument, hoping to make sense of it. They are talking about some woman, but I cannot catch her name. By the time I focus back on my siblings, Avery has calmed down a bit while Ethan glances at the door, waiting for them to stop. There is nothing I can do about my parents, but I want to try to comfort my siblings.

"You are not the problem," I firmly tell Avery, taking

her hand in mine. Avery looks at me with glossy eyes, and a tear rolls down her cheek. Just by looking at her, I know how she will respond.

"I am." She sniffles.

'They got in her sweet head.' I am thinking, wishing I could piece my sister back together with my words. Ethan shakes his head and softly repeats "no" to her. Things are so messed up—especially if Ethan is comforting instead of annoying. I hate this. I wonder if I can just open my window and leave. My mind starts to conjure all the ways to get out of here. Or maybe I can yell at my parents to stop, even though I would get yelled at back. Nothing is going to work. Instead of despairing, I grab the end of my sleeve and wipe Avery's tears. Without warning, Avery leaps towards me and embraces me.

"Sorry for putting so much on you," She apologizes, tears flowing steadily.

"No," I reassure, "We are displaying it out to figure it out."

She hugs me tighter, and I want to cry, too. Soon, Avery lets go and wipes her tears with her wrist.

"Do I look okay?" She asks.

"Beautiful as ever," I respond.

Ethan rolls his eyes and jokingly complains, "Alright, alright…" He smiles and pulls us up to leave.

Before we can make it through the door, Mama springs through the door and begins apologizing. None of us speak, letting Mama get out her apologies.

"I love you guys so much. I never thought that this

would happen. Forgive me for being a terrible Mama. I never wanted you guys to hear this!" She says, hugging us. The door bounces off the wall and hits Ethan's shoulder, and I hear a small 'ouch' from him. I glance over Mama's shoulder and see Papa shaking his leg and checking his watch unapologetically. "Look, kids, I never meant to make any of you cry," she says, sounding choked up.

"I have to let you guys go—" Mama regretfully says, letting us go as she checks the time. Papa interrupts her, speaking, "We're going to be late for lunch, dear." Mama looks behind her and back towards us. "Be good, all right? I love you. Your babysitter will be here soon. I must have a talk with your Pa' about something at lunch, so we will come to an agreement."

Everyone nods, and I look up towards her. Despite the arguing, she seems like she is okay. Things would be alright. Papa is no longer in sight, clearly having headed for the car. So, Mama leaves the room, us following, and goes into the junky garage into the white car we call our own. We stop at the door, watching them.

"I love you, kiddos," Mama says, smiling and waving while getting in the car.

Papa waves and starts the car. The smell of gas overwhelms me, so I go into the living room. The garage door opens, and I hear the car drive off. Then I hear the garage door close and the door to the garage, signaling my siblings having come back into the house. Avery sits beside me and looks at her hands while Ethan leans on the sage hallway wall, peering at us. Avery puts her head on my shoulder. I put my head on hers and close my eyes, trying to relax. It is not long before I hear a car drive into the driveway and a car door closing. Footsteps creep in front of our front door, and a knock follows.

"I'll get it." Ethan pipes up, jogging towards the door.

He opens the door, and there is Ms. Fredrick, our babysitter. Her full name is Becky Fredrick, but it's formal to call her Ms. Fredrick. As usual, she arrives in her Converse and jean shorts with leggings underneath. She would also wear some baggy jeans sometimes. She's not dressed up for the occasion, which is fair since we've got no plans for the day.

"Hey!" She greets as Ethan closes the door behind her, and she takes her shoes off. Avery turns with a smile, and I open my eyes and turn my head, too. She joins us on the couch, and Ethan sits in the chair beside the fireplace as usual. "So, what do we want to do today?" exclaims Ms. Fredrick.

"I have no idea," Ethan comments, kicking his feet on the tacky leaf-designed ottoman.

Avery looks like those cartoons where a bulb light clicks above her head as she suddenly offers, "Ah, how about we paint our fingernails?"

"Nah, I'm not doing that," Ethan responds after a sigh, soon chuckling.

"A puzzle?" Ms. Fredrick suggests.

"It's more like this is a puzzle. No, we don't have any," Ethan replies, scratching his head. Avery gets up, enters the storage closet, and moves some items around. We all watch her, curious to know what she's looking for.

"Aha!" She yells triumphantly as she pulls out a box with dust and blows it away.

The box displays a text saying 'Puzzle4Everyone!' or something cheesy like that. I am surprised by Avery's discovery. Avery walks to the coffee table and places the box on it. Ms. Fredrick opens the box, pulls out the puzzles, and dumps it on the table.

"Alrighty, kids, let's get to work!"

Ethan jumps up from the chair and sits down on the ground in front of the coffee table, about to get to work. We hear yet another knock at the door, so I excuse myself and get up to answer it. Through the glass, I see Nolan waiting patiently for someone to answer. I open the door, and Nolan gives me a brilliant smile with his pearly teeth.

"Hey, are you busy?" He asks.

I look behind me and see everyone waiting, so I answer, "A bit… Do you like puzzles?"

Nolan nods and verbally states, "Yeah, but I haven't done one since last summer."

"Come inside then!" I say, inviting him inside and closing the door behind him.

We walk into the living room. Before I can tell Nolan to sit and make himself comfortable, I notice Ms. Fredick staring at us. I tilt my head questioningly at her.

"Are you two… dating?" Ms. Fredricks inquires, looking us over.

Nolan and I look at each other, grimacing and shaking our heads. I make a funny expression like I am throwing up or gagging. Nolan rolls his eyes and laughs. That answers Ms. Fredrick's question, and she chuckles at our antics. With that behind us, we all sit on the ground and begin working on the puzzle. Like all puzzles, of course, it is tricky. Even with five people, it is so confusing, but this does not stop us from enjoying ourselves. We are having a fun time and joking around.

"How long have you been babysitting Londyn and her siblings?" Nolan asks.

"I actually do not know. I remember babysitting them when I was about fourteen, so... for about two years?" Ms. Fredrick responds, smiling.

Nolan nods in acknowledgment.

"Wow, look at all those years that have flown by," Ethan comments, shaking his head in disbelief.

I nod and chuckle at all the memories we had together. This puzzle is like piecing all those memories together and the ones longing to occur. Just like all the time that has gone by over the years, so has the time now.

It is now the afternoon, and Nolan has left to eat lunch with his grandma and said "goodbye" if he did not return afterward. Now, we all sit bored, so Ethan turns on the TV. Avery asks if we want anything to drink, and we all respond with a yes. Our mouths and throats are dry like a desert, and we have had nothing to drink during the hours we were working on the puzzle. Thankfully, Avery comes back swiftly with water and places it on the table. I drink the water as if I were about to die of dehydration or something. While I am gulping down water, Ms. Fredrick's phone buzzes, and we watch her face light up in shock as she checks it. I sit my bottle down and question her about what was wrong. Much to my surprise, she just shakes her head and goes into the other room.

"What was that about?" Avery asks as she raises an eyebrow and glances at the room Ms. Fredrick disappeared into.

I shrug, not having any answers, while we wait for the babysitter to return. Ethan is flipping through the channels on the TV, looking as if he is not worried about the situation. He momentarily stops on a news channel, yawning when they start talking about politics. I open my mouth to tell him to keep going, but soon, we hear a faint cry from the room, and I am starting to get really worried now. A blast of confusion and worry spreads across my face unintentionally. None of us managed to get to our feet to check before Ms. Fredrick comes back with a worried face and wide eyes, sniffling.

"What happened?" I ask as I stand up, eyes wide, too.

Ethan also stands up, accidentally knocking his water bottle over—though he could not have cared less in that moment as he goes to Ms. Fredrick. I am about to ask her again what happened when my attention is caught by the TV, which is now showing something about a white Honda. I do not fully process it before my phone suddenly vibrates with a news alert.

The headline reads, "Breaking News: Two people are hospitalized after a white Honda crashes into a local public service on W Fort Macon Rd."

My heart drops to my stomach. Ms. Fredick trips over a water bottle as she attempts to shut off the TV before the man on the screen can speak. Due to her tripping, she does not make it on time, and Kay is on the ground watching the TV reporter chatter away at an auto wreck. Everything I just read is being said. The man on the screen, with outstanding brown hair, begins to speak.

"We acknowledge a terrible auto wreck that happened today, where a white Honda crashed into a local public service building. Two people, as we speak, are being hospitalized right now. As of now, all we know is that they will be in the near hospital for quite some time due to their horrible injuries."

A shiver runs down my spine as I stumble over my words, "Is it just a coincidence?" My voice is barely above a whisper, but I am sure I was heard. Avery has wide eyes, tears filling them. On the TV, they display an image of what seems to look exactly like Mama and Papa on the screen, injured severely. I do not want to look at the gruesome details—and apparently, Ms. Fredrick does not want to watch anymore either as she turns off the TV. Avery breaks down in tears as Ethan tries to comfort her while trying not to cry like a baby. Ms. Fredrick rushes to the other room again. I rush to Avery, hugging her tightly. My mind is racing, and I can only focus on the smell of Avery's clean clothes and hair, which smells like coconut milk. I close my eyes, allowing hot tears to build up. During our bawling, Ms. Fredrick returns with a shaky request.

"P-Please, if you guys do not mind, go pack your bags…just in case."

Ethan turns to her and nods. I am taken aback that he did not ask for an explanation.

"I want to take something valuable from our parents to remind us of them- like they are with us." I quickly say.

Excusing myself and separating from my siblings, I go into my parent's bedroom while Ethan and Avery go into their bedrooms and grab their suitcases. I tug on the string to turn the ceiling fan's light on. I look behind me and fixate on a specific point. That drawer Papa had put that thick book in earlier. I open the drawer and see the notebook sitting innocently inside. It has 'Frank Scarlet' on the front, and a lock keeping it closed. My first thoughts are about how I need to find the key. I know the keys could be in his pocket or the car, but there is a chance they were in this house. Despite everything, I rush out of our parent's room and knock on Avery's door. She opens the door with fresh tears in her eyes.

"Yes, Lon?" She asks.

"Didn't Ma' say there was an attic?" I question.

Avery nods, and I smile.

"What are you smiling for?" she wonders, but I do not have time to discuss the details.

I call for Ethan. Time shifts. The next thing I know, we are standing at the door to the attic, about to head inside. It is dusty inside, and my nose scrunches up. This is truly a dusty, old attic, with light twinkling from the window, making the dust dancing about more noticeable.

I hear Ethan's voice echo as he exclaims, "You've got to see this!"

Ethan steps inside the attic first, and Avery follows with a "wow." I look over at Ms. Fredrick, who simply shakes her head and just tells us to be careful. I know she is indulging us to get our minds off everything potentially happening, and I am grateful. Turning back, I follow my siblings into the attic. Again, I am astonished by the dust floating about and covering everything. I do my best not to sneeze while looking around for a key. I cannot call my siblings' attention to it just yet... and fortunately, I do not have to ask for their help since I eventually notice something shimmering in the corner behind some cardboard boxes. To my relief, it is a key. Hopefully, it is the key, so I pick it up and put it in my pocket. Somewhere else in the attic, someone else makes a discovery.

"I found an old yearbook of Mama's," Ethan comments, tearing up again.

"Yeah, way to brighten the mood," Avery responds, scoffing.

"...You want to know somethin'? You are acting just like Papa." Ethan shoots back.

It gets silent.

"Don't you ever say that to me again," Avery states coldly, deciding to climb down before they start an intense argument.

Swallowing around the lump in my throat, I also leave the attic. It is the wise thing to do, too—besides, I only came to the attic to search for the key. Patting the lingering dust off my hands, I go back into our parents' room and close the door behind me. I take the key out of my pocket and put it in the hole to hopefully unlock it. When nothing happens at first, I frown, thinking it is not the right key… It takes a few times until I finally hear the click I wanted to. I open the journal to the front page and see a picture glued onto it, displaying Mama and Papa on a hiking trip.

At the bottom of the page, it says: "Summer of 2010: I miss that woman. I miss the way she laughed and smiled. I miss our lovely daughter, Lainey. But that woman had to marry someone anyway to, I suppose, "forget" about me. Now, it is Lainey Mackenzie. She still has my DNA. Though, I do not love Amanda anymore. No, that was just a season. I was so deep into that season that I forgot to take the Halloween décor and put up the Christmas decorations for Dahlia. I am not good at poetry, but oh well. I already had children with Amanda, so what is the point? I will just move and start somewhere else. Bye, Dahl."

I slam the journal shut at once before reading any more. My heart is racing, and my world feels like it's spinning. 'Should I have even read this?' I ponder. Do I have another sister they never told me about? I feel sick as I throw the journal aside and put my hands on my forehead, brushing my hair with my chubby fingers. I hear a knock and hide the journal behind me as Avery walks in.

"I know it's hard having both our parents in an auto

accident, but maybe let's take three photographs with all of us in it," Avery voices, attempting to sound optimistic.

I nod and look around the dead room. The beige walls turn to grey, and the pop of color from Mama's necklace, which she usually puts on her nightstand, is gone. Instead of being there, it is on her neck… and on the ground with her. The thought makes me want to tear up again. I turn away and look behind me, seeing the journal.

"Uhm… do you think they have three photographs of all of us?" I manage to ask.

Avery walks towards the dresser that is against the wall in front of the bed, pulls out a drawer, and shuffles through it. I watch her work distractedly, fingers brushing against the journal.

"He should," Avery starts. "He always took photos and recordings of us at Christmas or late summer whenever his old stupid camera worked." She opens a drawer and closes it back with wide eyes, and I become concerned.

"What'd you… see?" I question, wondering if she had uncovered a secret as well.

"Nothing, this is just the clothing drawer," she answers, shaking her head.

"Oh…" I respond, still taken aback by her response.

"Aha, there it is!" she says, looking at the nightstand behind and to my left.

I shift the journal to my right so she does not notice it. Though, it does not appear to matter. She only has eyes for what's in front of her as she places herself in front of the nightstand. She looks through some photographs with all of us in there. She starts to tear up again.

"Do we really have to go?" she asks aloud.

"I know..." I say, looking at my socks and then the wall with tears in my eyes.

"I know I haven't lived here all my life, but now this is home." Avery murmurs.

"What?" I am startled at what she said.

"We lived in Tennessee before moving here when you were born." She fills in.

"Why?" I wonder.

She shrugs and responds, "Papa said to get away from horrible memories and the past that he didn't want to remember there."

"He lied to Ms. Price a—"

"I know," Avery interrupts and nods, tears sliding down her cheek. I look beside me at the journal. "Well, I'm going to put this in my bag for us, okay?" She mumbles, holding up the photographs. All I can do is nod, and as she walked towards the door, I shift the journal behind me, still wanting to keep it from her sight. She then pokes her head in and asks, "Is there something you want to tell me? I am always available."

For a moment, I think she knows about the journal, but I only shake my head at her offer and question. She nods and closes the door. I sit there in the cool, dead-silent room. I question how everything happened so fast. The day had started out poorly with Mama and Papa arguing, but things had picked up when Nolan came over. I cannot help but ask myself how everything ended up like this.

Soon, my mind spirals and leads me to ask myself one specific question: Am I the problem? I am… I think I am. If I were not born, we would not have moved here. The journal and Avery's words make me feel like this is true. I do not think Lainey would have happened if she is who I think she could be. I do not think any of this would happen. Avery said she was the "problem," but I think it is clear who is the problem: me.

I will not tell anyone about this—I swear I will never. My body starts to shake, and I shake my head to myself as I try to find resolve. I will not tell anyone about this dumb journal. A tear rolls down my cheek, and I start to sniffle. I try hard not to cry; I try to hold it in. It is futile. The next thing I know, I am crying. I work hard to be silent as I sit there on my Mama and Papa's bed, crying like a baby. The only thing I know to do is to pray to God. So, I do. Eventually, my mind goes blank, and I start crying again.

"God, I can't do this," I murmur under my breath, unfolding my hands and placing them on my face.

I sit for a few minutes, trying to get myself together and think of my next move. Finally, I decide to just snatch the journal and put it in my backpack for my own. So, I hide it under my shirt and turn off the light, sneaking out of my parents' room and into mine. I shut the door and shove the journal in my backpack. I zip up my backpack and just sit on my bed. I just sit there in my room and think about those bodies that were my Mama and Papa. I cannot believe it; I mean, is this real? I think for a second that I am dreaming, but no, I just need to wake up. I just do not know how to escape from this nightmare.

Chapter Four

TELL EVERYONE I KNOW THAT I WILL MISS THEM

Atlantic Beach, North Carolina, June 21, 2018

It is early in the morning, and it has just stopped raining. The sheets and covers that were once warm are now cold. I wake up with a slight headache and puffy eyes from last night's event. I cried and cried last night until I eventually fell asleep. There is little light from my window since it is cloudy and misty from the previous night's rain. I did not want to get up or begin my day. As I lie in bed, all I remember is Mama coming in and waking me up gently. I took it all for granted. Why was I so selfish? But I cannot sit and wallow for long since my mind reminds me that there is something important to do…

For a brief moment, I had forgotten. Today is the day that we will move. I feel like each day is just passing by, and I am not doing much. For the past few days, the only things I have been doing are packing and crying over and over, which is exhausting! I am not even communicating with anyone. I do not want to visit my parents, but at the same time, I do. I just do not want to see them and start crying like a baby. Despite the day's plans, I am still in my bed, listening to all these thoughts race in my head like some marathon. I toss and turn, wanting the sheets to just devour me already. I do not even care if they are cold anymore.

"Lord," I whisper under my shaking breath as I am about to sob. "Why couldn't you have taken me last night?"

I sniffle a bit, take a breath, and shake my head. I start to think logically despite my fears, reminding myself my parents are still living and are being hospitalized now. I mean, I have not gotten a lot of answers or anything about this matter. I do know that Mama is not doing well right now. Though she is safe and in great care, the doctors are trying their best. I always knew Mama as a strong woman who could battle through anything, but this time... This time is different. I force the thought from my head, knowing it would only depress me.

It will be a couple of hours before our grandparents come up and take us with them. So, I need to prepare myself during this time. Sitting straight, I look around my room and turn on the lamp. My room. The room I suppose I moved into when I was a baby. I grew up here, and I do not want to lose it. I do not want to lose any of the things I have gained here. I start to think about my friends, knowing I do not want to lose them either. I do not want to lose anyone. Before I know it, I am crying again, muffling my sound so my siblings in their room do not hear me bawl like some crybaby.

When I manage to pull myself together, I check my phone. I forgot to charge it last night, and I know my grandparents would hog the outlet in the car to have their GPS on. I dread smelling the smoke in the van. My nose scrunches up, and my eyebrows narrow slightly just at the thought. Well, I suppose my phone is all right for now. It is too early for any of my siblings or neighbors to be up this Thursday morning without school in session. Somewhere, a group of girls, maybe Helen, Makayla, and Kourtney, might pull an all-nighter during a sleepover. If I were not to be moving right now, I would have had a sleepover for my birthday today. I think I would have invited Nolan and Hailee, too. My mind is bogged down with all these thoughts, and I try to empty my head and find something else to focus on.

I type in my password and open my phone to the home screen. I scroll through the digital home screen pages, tap on a random app, and scroll through the reels. Although the videos attempt to brighten my mood, my mood just would not light. It just stays there like a candle on a bedside table, unlit. No flame on the wick. That is how my mood has been ever since that incident occurred. But I do manage to snicker at some of the videos shown, unable to resist their charms completely. I keep scrolling through social media mindlessly, able to shut off my brain for a while. I just scroll and get sucked in. I am involved in reels and media, absorbed in a digital life. Now, I do not know where I was or who I was.

Then I blink and look around, reality sinking back in. Oh, that is right. I am Londyn McKay Scarlet, who is thirteen today. I look around my room and notice a stain on the wall that stayed there ever since that one time I was seven and spilled blue raspberry lemonade by accident. I chuckle a bit at the thought, but truly, I want to cry again. I will forever miss this place and the memories it has. Oh, all the sweet memories and remembrances. I was so lost in reels and memories that I did not notice the time. The sun is already out and shining through my window. This signals to me that my day probably should begin.

To be sure, I check the time, and it shows me it is 8:56 A.M. I gasp, hopping out of bed, and get everything ready for the long road trip. I collect the suitcase beside my bed and rush to get my favorite pair of shoes: white, dirty Crocs. They have traveled with me everywhere, and there is no way I will accidentally leave them behind. As I'm packing up, I get a notification from an app I almost never use. I plop back onto my bed and open my phone to check, taking note of the twenty-four notifications I never really focused on getting out of the way because what if I need to remember them? Once I am who knows what number of all twenty-four notifications, I see the latest notification is a message sent from Hailee. I do not want to open it and leave her on read if I choose not to respond.

The message says: "Hey, I wanted to check on you and see how you were doing. You have not reached out to me or anyone. Oh, and happy birthday!"

I frown and sigh, murmuring, "I know."

What a mood switch. But this does remind me of something. It is insane how reading something from a book, article, poem, or any writing source can affect your mood—like it controls you just from reading those words. Our minds just cannot tell reality apart from delusion or fiction. I do not need anything else to ruin my mood, knowing reminders will only bring me down. With another sigh, I remove all my notifications and turn off my phone. Sitting up, I try not to think of anything at all. For a while, I am successful as my mind is blank, and my body is still. Minutes ticking by…

I sit in my cold, quiet room, staring blankly around me. 'Is this how it is always going to be?' I ponder, realizing this is the only remaining thought left in my head. I have not done jack squat for the past few days. I feel like I will be like this forever. 'Forever,' I think, thoughts beginning to flood my mind again. My mind jumps around, wandering off again, and I think, 'No, I will not and will not be like this forever.' I am certain this season will end like any other, just like when Lemonade, our Labrador Retriever, died. I was sad for the most part, but then I started to like drawing. That got my mind off things bit by bit… Soon, I snap back into reality, back to the present, and finally get a grip on my thoughts. I recall what I was trying to do. I must get things packed and ready for the long road trip ahead. Moving about, I try to check all my luggage to see if anything is missing or if there is anything else I want to take. When one fits all of their clothes inside one large suitcase, it is difficult to dive, search around, and see if anything is missing.

I soon hear a gentle knock at my door and wonder who it is. Taking a breath, I advance towards the door, leaving my suitcase behind me like a sad puppy awaiting. I sneak a peek by opening the door a bit. When I see sad hazel eyes peering back at me, I know I have to let her in. I open the door, and Avery leaps towards me and embraces me. Her face nuzzles into my hair as she spills her thoughts.

"Londyn, I don't want to go," She sobs, echoing my feelings.

My grip tightens as she shares her feelings, and the dam breaks as I begin to weep and wail. Our pain seems never-ending, and I realize someone is missing. I shift and see a glimpse of Ethan in the doorway, with his arms folded, looking at the cold, hard ground. I cannot tell if he is crying or not with his head down, but eventually, he joins our embrace.

"I know what role I'm supposed to play, but," Avery starts to cry even harder after saying this, "I do not know if I can take it." I can feel her legs weaken as we let her go, and she plummets to the floor. "Lord!" She shrieks as she shakes her head.

She clasps her hands together, and we all do the same. I look at Ethan with a forceful smile, and he cries openly. Sniffling, I sit with Avery, and Ethan does, too. Avery prays, and we join in following every word she speaks. Soon, she is overcome with her emotions once more, beginning to cry, and we say a quick "amen" to end it.

"Avery," Ethan murmurs. Avery looks up at him with tears down her cheek, a red face, and eyes filled with salty tears. "You're doing a great job." She almost cries even harder, but she tries to contain herself, wanting to hear more of what he has to say. "I know everything is so hard right now, but we come from an extensive line of strong people. If you have a bit of faith…" He then pulls his hand up and squints his pointer finger and thumb together to symbolize a small amount of something. "Everything will work out."

Avery nods as she hugs him tight.

"It a-always works o-out in the end," I say with a bit of stuttering between some words.

Ethan opens his right arm to signal me to join them. I join in and try to smile as he hugs us ever so warmly. We sit there for quite a while, and I eventually doze off in my sibling's arms. I do, however, feel one of them carry me to bed. The cold sheets cover me once more as I am lulled back to sleep... And the next thing I know, I am being awoken by my grandma.

"We need to get on the road!" She exclaims with a smile I know is on her lips. "We got a surprise for you at the house."

Well, despite my apprehension, her words pique my interest. I know it is my birthday, so maybe that is the nature of the surprise, a surprise birthday party, or whatever it has to do with a birthday. Opening my eyes wider, I roll over to the opposite side of the bed and see Grandma standing there with a wrinkled smile and eyes. I only see Grandma and Grandpa once a year, so to stay with them, potentially forever, will feel so different. I know their house... I know where the guest bedrooms and the bathrooms are, but I do not know every crack and cranny—not like I know my house.

My thoughts get jumbled as Grandma tosses the sheets off my cold, still body, just as Mama used to joke around. I get up, groaning in pain from my sharp headache. Grandma gives me a worried look and pulls me into a hug. Over Grandma's shoulder, I see Grandpa and Ethan picking up my stuff and taking it out of the room with the other belongings. I hug Grandma back, needing comfort, and she places a loving, wet kiss on my forehead. I cringe a bit, but I do not want to show it. She would always do this. I did not notice Avery hovering by the bed until Grandma moved away from me to kiss her cheek. I watch, hoping the comfort helps my sister.

"My babies are going to be safe with us," Grandma says, looking at us both while her lips curve into a comforting smile.

"Did you get any news from the hospital?" I ask, interrupting the silence. Grandma frowns and looks as if she is about to weep.

"Yes," she says in a simple response.

"Please tell us." Avery pleads.

Grandma fidgets and sighs before telling us, as if it were bad. Is it bad, though? 'Please, Lord, I cannot take any more…' I think to myself.

Grandma finally says, "Your Mom is not in the best shape right now. They are optimistic for her. All we can do is hope she is strong enough." Avery is stunned by these words, and her mouth hangs as her eyebrows swoop sadly. "I'm so sorry," Grandma says as if she is about to cry. Her lips twitch, and so do her eyebrows, looking just as saddened as Avery's.

'Lord…' I think one more time. 'Why?' I think again.' Why us?' I shut my eyes, and my breath quivers as I exhale. I open my eyes, and Avery just shakes her head.

"I'm just going to meet you guys in the car after this luggage gets in the van."

She stomps out after her words, and I hear a suitcase roll on the solid wood floor. I turn to Grandma with the only lamp shining on her, making a mystical view.

"Grandma," I gear up to ask. "What about Papa?"

She turns to me quickly just as I say this. She shakes her head just as Avery did and shrugs.

"I don't know, babydoll…" she says, a glistening tear traveling down her wrinkly cheek. "I do not know." She repeats.

This only makes my yearning grow worse. I just want to leave this place already, but at the same time, I do not. I just want to go back in time and relive the days when they were not injured severely in the hospital. I want to hug Mama again. I want her to braid my hair again. I want her to wash my hair like she did when I was six. I want to see her warm smile as she cooks a hot meal on a frigid day.

I want her again. Please, Lord, I want her back. I want her to embrace me and tell me, "It's going to be okay," when I make a mistake or scrape my knee on the pavement. I want to watch movies with all my siblings as I hear my parents pop popcorn in the kitchen and mix some hot chocolate, and we make silly forts that eventually end up falling on us. I want her back. I want everything back. I know I am not out of this house yet or even on the road, but I want this home to feel like home again. It is not the same without them. It will never ever feel like home again here. I finally snap out of my thoughts and get up.

"Oh," I speak, feeling utterly lost.

I cannot recognize my room anymore. All my posters are gone, and so are my jewelry, clothes, shoes, and everything else—except for the major things, like my bed, dresser, table, lava lamp, fairy lights, etc. These are the only things you can recognize my room with, but everything else that makes me, me, is gone and in the bags or suitcase I am going to bring with me.

Grandma leaves the room, signaling me to follow. I grab my phone and drink, get up, and head for the door. Before I close the door one last time, I take a good look at my room. I look at the stain again, the dresser I always bump my hip into, my closet with a creaky door, my comfortable bed that was once warm, my nightstand which held my notebook filled with art, my fairy lights which flicker sometimes, and my lava lamp which I turn on every now and then. I start to tear up again and sniffle.

"I'll miss you," I murmur.

Grandma had already left, but I suddenly sense a presence behind me. Turning around, it is Ethan. I close my door and read the sign on the door, which says, 'Londyn's bedroom, knock before entry!' on it. I chuckle at it, but at the same time, I find my eyes filling with moisture.

"Are you ready, Lon?" Ethan questions as he flings his bag over his shoulder. I nod in agreement, and he advances towards the door out of the hallway. I walk down the quiet hallway.

I look at him with teary eyes and ask, "Can I look around a bit before we leave?"

"I don't see why not," Ethan responds, nodding.

I first go to the living room and take a good look at it. Everything I see brings up memories, the sweet memories of where we used to watch movies, build forts, and the incident. I remember when I saw the gruesome news on the television about my parents. That memory overpowers all the happy times in this moment. I want to vomit as I hold my stomach, about to cry. As much as I want to look at the rest of the house, I need to leave before I become too overwhelmed by this. It is the wisest choice for me right now. I go towards the door and open it, stepping outside as the coastal winds fill my lungs. I see Ethan getting in the van, and I close the door behind me. I lock it, and I huff out a big sigh. I walk towards the van, but I look behind me just one more time. Just one more time when I can enjoy this breeze and the sun shining proudly upon me. Just one more time when I could enjoy the beach. Just one more time, I can call this place home.

Just one more time...

Turning around, I open the car door and hop inside unwillingly. I close it shut and place my drink in the cup holder. I can smell the cigarette smoke inside and cough, but I do not want to be too disrespectful. I hand the keys to Grandma, and she takes them.

“Alrighty now, is everyone settled? No restroom? Go before it is too late,” Grandpa says, starting the car up as we hear it crank up and bounce a bit. It is silent. “Alright, I’ll take that as a no.” He comments, looking in the mirror at us.

Grandpa had a small beard he was proud of and showed it, too. I look over his features briefly before dropping my eyes to folded hands in my lap. As I hear more words coming from the front of the van, I look up again.

“Hey, kids,” He murmurs, looking down at his dirty hands from the woodwork. We look at him curiously at what he has to say, and so does Grandma. “I know it’s difficult going through this, but we’ll go through it together.” He looks at us with piercing blue eyes and a sympathetic smile plastering his face. His eyes wrinkled, and so did the end of his smile. “It is so hard knowing my daughter and son-in-law are in the hospital. But let us have faith, okay?” The whole car stays silent once again, giving an awkward tension floating about in the air. “Sorry...” He murmurs, frowning, then starts to drive out of the driveway.

I try to look back and pass the luggage to the burning

memory. We drive along the road, and I cannot see it anymore—the place I called home.

"Hey," I speak, thinking of my parents in the hospital. I tap on the back of Grandpa's seat.

"What's up?" Grandpa asks me, glancing through the rearview mirror at me.

"Can we go visit the hospital?" I ask with my heart racing.

I am terrified. I do not want to see my parents, especially Mama, in a horrible condition, but if that is what it takes to see them before I leave, then I will. His eyes soften, and I see his eyes getting watery.

"Sure, kiddo, we will."

I endeavor to smile, but it just does not happen despite my best efforts. The car ride is silent again, and I pop in my earbuds to listen to music on my phone. I look out the window at the busy streets that flood with people going to work or others walking on the beach. I watch other cars pass by, red, white, black, grey, blue, and even a small yellow car. I watch one woman kiss a guy on the cheek as she holds his hand. A smile finds its way onto my face just by seeing this. I look to my left to see Avery scrolling on her phone endlessly and Ethan in a deep sleep. I take my earbuds out and hear Ethan snore, making me snicker. Avery even looks up and smiles.

"He is in one deep sleep, isn't he?" She whispers while our grandparents listen.

I nod and look back outside again, my cheek resting on my fist. I look at the cloudy sky and passing buildings.

I challenge myself by counting the houses, buildings, and people just for the fun of it. It does not last long, as thoughts start to flood back in, hitting me with a realization: I did not tell anyone goodbye.

"I didn't get to tell anyone I'm moving," I gasp loudly to my grandparents, still low enough so Ethan wouldn't wake up.

I was so lost in my own sadness that I did not take the time to let my friends know I was leaving. I did not get to say goodbye to anyone.

"They'll notice you're gone," Grandma says, glancing at me.

"What is that supposed to mean?" I ask.

"It means they will notice. You are the sunshine to everyone's cloudy day. Why can't you see this?" she says, her smile soon fading into a frown. I look outside. "See? It is so cloudy, but when you are with your friends, it is so sunny and merry." She responds.

I know it is a coincidence, but I still do not know if I can fully believe her. I peek one last time outside to see the dark clouds. She does have a point. 'Do not be full of yourself.' I begin to think these dark thoughts again. Why do I have these thoughts? I try to think great of myself, but it crumbles into tiny pieces of insecurity and self-hatred like glass. Why do I have this tiny voice? It tells me lies, but again, they are truths. I am just picking out the ugly parts of myself and downing myself on that. I can never find any good parts. I can never find any pretty parts of me. I am so lost in my self-loathing that I do not realize we have arrived at the hospital until the car stops moving.

"Okay, we are here," Grandpa says, unbuckling his seatbelt.

I follow his lead, unbuckling my seatbelt, as do Avery and Grandma. Ethan does not move, still asleep. I envy him for a few seconds, watching the rise and fall of his chest.

"Wake him up for us, please, Avery," Grandma suggests as she turns to look at them.

Avery shakes him gently. She is unsuccessful in her first attempt. So, she shakes him again but with more force. He eventually wakes up and lets out a loud groan. I smile a little, watching him try to shake off sleep.

"Are we there?" He asks as he rubs his eyes with a sleepy tone.

"No, we're at the hospital to visit Mama and Papa," she answers.

Ethan turns to look at the enormous building before us and mumbles, "Ah, okay," as he reluctantly pulls the blanket from himself. I open the car door, and our grandparents follow. I get nervous and shake slightly as my feet hit the hard ground, doing my best to stand without wobbling. I hear Avery close the car door behind us, and I know I have to keep moving forward. We walk all the way from the lot to the hospital's interior. I look around at the cold, dull waiting room with people wandering about. I look down at my shoes while the adults talk. Ethan tries to hold his yawns as the silence grows bigger. And larger. And quieter—until Grandma tugs on my shirt, signaling us to follow and go to the assigned room.

We walk down the white hallways which lingered with even more silence. Our heavy shoes hit the cold, hard ground and echo throughout the hallway. I follow my grandparents closely as I do not know which room we are going to. I am doing my best to gather my courage, but my body still shakes with every step I take.

"Ah, here," says Grandpa. Before we can go any further, Grandpa holds us back by questioning our decision. "Are you guys sure?" he asks as he puts his hand on the door handle.

I nod my head, being extremely sure. 'Please, I want to see Ma and Pa,' I think as I yearn for him to open the door and let me in. Avery whispers a quiet "yes." Ethan thinks long and hard about this. He sighs as he gives in and nods.

"Okay…" Grandpa responds, sounding rather choked up.

The colossal and heavy door swings open as Grandpa holds it for us to go inside. As we head in, I see Mama and Papa on separate white beds, both awake. I immediately notice Mama's heart rate does not look too good. Avery rushes towards Mama and falls to her knees beside her.

"Mama…" She says in a hushed yet worried tone.

Grandpa walks over to his son-in-law's bedside and begins to sob. This is the first time I have ever seen this bulky, strong man cry. 'You were right, Mama. Even strong people can cry,' I think distractedly. Like Ethan, who is crying on Grandma's shoulder right now. I stand beside Mama and Avery as Mama slowly and weakly turns her head towards us.

"I love you." she rasps, trying to form a frail smile towards us.

A tear travels its merry way down her cheek with clear direction—it knows exactly where it is going. It falls on her sweet lips. Avery bawls and crumbles. I realize my body is still shaking, but I open my mouth, needing to express my feelings before I, too, am seized by emotions.

"Mama," I suggest.

"Lon?" She asks, giving me a warm but weak smile.

"Can you get well for me?" I beg, beginning to sob.

She tries to nod her head as she lies in the cold sheets that gracefully cover her. "Yes, dear, look now. I haven't had the best heart. You understand?" she speaks.

"What? You are the sweetest person I know!" I interrupt.

"No, silly, I have a weak heart, always had one. I have an issue." She blurts before I jump to more conclusions. Now everything made sense.

"Ah, but you're going to get better, right?" I ask.

She is silent—silent as a mouse. Then she frowns. She looks around the room, trying not to make things awkward.

"Ma'?" Avery asks. "Well, are you?" she asks again, getting up with a worried look and wild eyes as if she had seen a ghost.

"I'm so sorry." Mama apologizes, crying again, and she turns to me. "I forgot to tell you, my sweet baby, happy birthday." She says, giving me a warm smile before fluttering her tired eyes. "I love you, my children, I always had and will. When I reach heaven, I will ask God to send angels down to look after you-"

"Ma,' stop that talk!" Avery hollers as she begins to bawl again.

Papa is asleep now. My heart beats faster as Mama's heart rate slows down. The machine reading makes my stomach knot.

"Mama!" I shout as two nurses come rushing in. I had not noticed Grandma pushing the red button on the off-white wall.

"Please, go." One of the nurses orders.

"No!" Ethan tries to refuse as Grandpa pushes him out.

My head spins, and so does my world. Hot tears drip from my eyes and down my face, and saliva fills my mouth when I start to speak up.

"Is she going to be okay?" I ask before I get pushed out, and the door shuts on us.

'Why? What had we done to deserve something so horrid?' I demand to know in my mind. No answers reach me, and I find no comfort or relief. I want to talk to Mama just a bit longer before I leave. But Papa… I do not want to see him, or I will throw up knowing how he feels about her and us. The words from the journal swirl in my mind as I stare at the closed door in front of me, willing it to open and let me see Mama once more.

"Lord, oh Lord…" Grandma says, putting her hand

on her head and sobbing.

"I think it would be best to go." Ethan inputs, looking at all of us with eyes flooded with sorrow.

Avery nods, and Grandpa leads the way to the parking lot. It is quiet as we make our way. None of us speak, and it almost feels as if the hospital itself is muffled and muted. Soon, we're outside again, reaching the van. We open the doors, and all hop back inside, our heads filled with headaches and trauma. It is back to the smell of cigarette smoke inside a junk van filled with luggage and road trip snacks.

"Is she going to be okay?" asks Ethan.

Grandma glances at him. It is silent before she says, "Yeah, she will be better than ever."

I do not get what she implies as I lazily look out the window, revisiting everything that occurred. The van cranks up, pulling out of the parking lot to continue our journey, and we are soon on the road in busy traffic. Cars honk and people grow tired and irritated—and so do I. Fidgeting in my seat, I try to get comfortable, knowing this is going to be a long ride. Soon, I find myself dozing off with my phone in my right hand and my head on the car window. It is a peaceful but tiresome sleep. I can hear the muffled sound of my grandparents talking and Avery scrolling on her phone, eating some snacks. I lull myself into a deep sleep and begin to dream of something.

In my dream, it is me, Hailee, and Coraline going down a tunnel. The tunnel is dark, and every noise echoes as we step closer to the blinding light. Ahead, there is nothing but white light shimmering. I then see a faded face smiling. To me, it looks like Coraline's smile because of her big teeth. Next, I see a vivid memory of Hailee and me having our sleepovers as children, where we built forts and stole some cookies in my bedroom, falling asleep peacefully after the mayhem. The visions are comforting, but the dream ends as I wake up.

I wake up as the van is preparing to turn into the parking lot of a gas station. As we stop for gas, Grandpa hops out to pump. Ethan slams the door to go inside the local gas station with Grandma. Avery leans on me with a blanket wrapped around her as she reads a book. This was peaceful, I think, yawning softly. I rub my face a little, staring at Avery.

"Finally getting back into reading, huh?" I ask to interrupt the silence and repeal any awkwardness.

"No, my phone is just dead," She responds.

"Of course..." I say, rolling my eyes, and grab a bag of chips. The bag is quite loud, and I hear Avery groan.

"Can't you open that quieter?" She demands, closing her book aggressively.

"Here, then you try it, little miss perfect!" I counter, throwing the bag towards her.

"I'm sick of the name-calling, so quit it." She says, tearing the bag open.

I frown as she shoves the bag in my face and gets up, no longer leaning on me. She is obviously annoyed, her eyebrows furrowed and screaming irritation. I turn over by the window and sigh. I did not want to eat anymore after that. It would just make things awkward. I had spoken to keep things from getting awkward, yet here we are. I do not want this to fester.

"Hey, look—" I begin.

"I don't want to hear it." She cuts me off with a clear, angry tone.

I sigh and keep my distance to avoid messing with her more. Now, the tension has mounted. We both jolt in surprise when Grandpa eventually gets back into the van after fueling it with gas. Grandma and Ethan also return, getting back into the van after buying some useful things and gadgets from the store.

"Alright, you all ready? We are about an hour away from the house," Grandpa says enthusiastically, frowning.

We all sit in silence as Grandpa, once again, starts the van. We start to advance and ride toward the open main road, where cars fly past each other. We then swerve and listen to Siri speak her commands loudly for our ears. Grandma turns on the radio to a country hit to fill the silence. The tension in the car shrinks a little with the noise. As we drive, I hope I did not miss the sign for when you entered Tennessee. My mind and gut are filled with guilt as I look over to Avery, who still seems slightly annoyed as she reads her book. I tap at her shoulder gently, and she gives me a curious look.

"I am sorry," I murmur, feeling some relief when she gives me a smile and closes her book, placing it in her bag.

"No, I apologize for creating this very unnecessary argument in the first place." She whispers, straightening her back.

Overall, everything is forgiven. I am relieved, not wanting to fight with Avery. With everything going on, we need to band together. A raised voice soon pulls me from my thoughts.

Grandma exclaims, "Ah, there it is!"

"What happened?" Ethan questions with confusion.

"Happy birthday to you!" Grandpa sings, giving me a warm glance. Grandma smiles and turns in her seat.

They sing me happy birthday and give me my used-to-be favorite cake when I was younger. I say a small thank you as I receive their small cake. I want to savor the cake, so I place it in my bag. Although I appreciate their efforts, it does not feel like my birthday at all. It simply does not feel right without my parents. I look at my chunky fingers, and then I look outside at the passing cars. I think: 'Everyone driving along this road has a story. Behind that story is them. Everything they love, go through, and create makes them them. It absolutely blows my mind to think just that… I do not think I care enough.'

Chapter Five

WHAT MAKES YOU SPECIAL?

Cookeville, Tennessee, August 8, 2018

My alarm on my phone shakes me awake and beeps thunderously. I click "snooze" as I do not want to be awakened. I did not want to begin my day. The testing for my new school was already hard enough! This summer, all I did was scroll on my phone, and scroll, and scroll, and scroll. Now that I think of it, it does sound depressing. I mean, I did not have my bike to ride, and plus, it would not feel the same as the beach. I dive back into my sheets, pulling the covers over my head. 'I miss the beach.' I think to myself, lips pouting unintentionally.

I miss the wind blowing in my face and caressing my hair. I miss Galena watching from her stand. I miss everything, but most of all, I miss Nolan. I miss that time at the beach with him and how my heart would flutter when he spoke in that raspy voice. I miss his laughter and how he acted and expressed himself when discussing his favorite things. I hope that he meets and gets along well with people there. I hope he talks about me like he does when he talks about the things he likes. I do not even have his number, any trace of our meeting, or of even knowing him. Now, it feels as if he was all just a memory. Now, it just feels like everything is unreal. It all happened so fast and unrealistically, and I just cannot believe it.

Things had certainly been shaky. My birthday here could have been better. But I know I will be quite all right if I have my family and myself. As all these thoughts race through my mind, blending together, I soon fall back into slumber. It is not a long and peaceful sleep, though. Sadly, moments later, Avery shakes me awake.

"We're going to be late!" She exclaims over and over.

I blink at her groggily, taking in her appearance. She has mascara and a bit of lip gloss on and is wearing nice clothing. 'Oh no,' I think as my wide eyes search across the room for something to do first. One thing I do not want to do on the first day is to be late! I cannot think straight, hopping out of bed quickly, and Avery gets out of my way as she grabs her backpack and rushes out the door. My heart beats loudly in my chest and ears. I search through the closet to find some decent clothes to wear. I change fast as I rush towards the bathroom to begin and end my routine rapidly. I wish I could take my time, but this is what I get for trying to grab a few more minutes of sleep.

As I apply mascara and perfume, I hear Grandma

saying she will start the family van. I put everything back as it was and look into the mirror again before leaving the bathroom and slamming the door shut. I scurry through the hallway, running into my room to grab my backpack and phone. I turn on my phone and mute the ringer so it would not be disruptive and get me into trouble. I open the door and leave the bedroom, unsure of the house's layout. This place is not home, and seeing it briefly forces my mind back... Everything reminds me of my parents. Everything is starting to remind me of the incident and that car wreck.

Knowing there is no time to fall apart, I put the second strap over my left shoulder and walk out of the house. I look at the dark grey family van that took me from home to this place. Steeling myself, I march over to the van, not stopping until standing outside it. Unsure of where to sit in the vehicle, I open the car door to the seats behind the front ones and slide in beside Avery and Ethan, shutting the door.

The smell of the unforgettable cigarette smoke inflates my lungs, and I breathe it out like a flood. The van starts, and it is unsettlingly quiet. Grandma notices this and takes it into her own hands by turning on the radio. A good hit seeps through the speakers, and while we normally dance, we just sit in silence as music rings in our ears. Though the music blasts and dances around in the car, the silence remains between people. The ride continues regardless. I look out the window and soon see the vast middle school that awaits me. We are pulling up and into the parking lot before I feel ready.

"Alright, Londyn. Have a great first day. We will take pictures when we get home," Grandma says, giving me a great smile.

I try to smile back and glance at Avery and Ethan before my eyes settle on Avery.

"Named after you, huh?" I say, remembering the name of my school: Avery Trace Middle School.

Avery rolls her eyes and smiles for once after the incident. I smile, real this time, because of that. I hop out of the car nervously and try to shake it off while I grab my backpack and pull it over my shoulder to let it hang. I close the door and watch the van drive away. I take a deep breath in and out... I try to calm down, but my racing thoughts interfere with my attempt to chill out. I turn around to the enormous school ahead of me. I walk into the building with my head down, scanning my schedule repeatedly until I bump into someone. Shoot... I stress. Not on my first day- are you stupid! I think to myself and feel my cheeks rising bright red in embarrassment. I glance up at the person I bumped into, hoping for an adult like a teacher or someone less likely to give me trouble.

Instead of a teacher, it is a tall eighth grader with long curly hair and pale skin like a vampire grimacing at me. If she raises her lips even more with this grimace, I think I might just see her fangs. I did not initially notice a girl beside her until the other girl whispered something into the vampire's ear while glaring at me. Was she talking about me? And on my first day, too? I quickly say sorry and walk around them, trying to ignore what just happened. I walk inside the school and see a wonderful entrance.

"Okay…" I murmur aloud as I review my paper to see where to go.

I also see in my peripheral vision the girls walking past me from earlier. Are all the students like this? I mentally question, trying not to frown. I walk into the commons, which is situated across the Y.M.C.A. Moving forward, I walk in there with a bunch of students and sit beside one of the many people. She has dark skin and curly black hair. As I keep looking, I quickly realize she is pretty. I notice she has long, pink fake nails applied and a wide smile when she talks to her friends. Not wanting to seem creepy, I look away from her and try to look at everyone long enough to get accustomed to their features. I am trying to imprint the newness of everything and everyone into my head, hoping it'll help me relax—though it's not working so far.

I check my phone quickly to see it is already 7:42 am. I know dismissal starts at 7:45 am, so I still have a little time to look around more. Like at my last school, I notice how every student is bunched up in a group. I know it sounds silly, like some High School Musical stuff, but it looks like it varies depending on their popularity and interests. I notice a group similar to volleyball, soccer, and many other sports. I see a vast group of guys on their phones laughing loudly. I am guessing that they are jocks since I spy their big and fancy shoes with jerseys and hoodies from last year. But just as I scan everyone and give them my opinion internally, the bell rings for dismissal.

My heart beats fast again, and I start shaking like a wet cat out of the rain. I prayed that today would go smoothly over the last few days—but I have already hit a stumbling block. My first class is math. With a long sigh, I trail down the long and dreadful hallways as I continuously review and analyze my schedule repeatedly. I will be sure to look in front of me this time so I do not make the same mistake as I did earlier. I groan and cringe at the idea. Just as I find and enter the classroom, the tardy bell rings. 'Phew,' I think. I have dodged a bullet, but not entirely.

The math teacher stands up from his desk with a ruler in his hand. He is a tall gentleman with a small white beard and light skin. He has a short haircut. Looking him over, I would have thought this man would have been in his 40s or late 30s. I do not get to muse long about him, though. My heart drops to my stomach as he assigns everyone a seat except for me. He looks at his attendance, then over to me, glances at his paper once more, and then eventually settles his gaze solely on me.

"I don't see you on my sheet. Are you in the right class, ma'am?" he asks, putting on a small pair of glasses and analyzing the schedule thoroughly.

"Yes, sir," I say, stumbling over some words and wiping my sweaty palms discreetly.

He nods with firm eyebrows and calls the central office from the telephone on the off-white wall. I stand there nervously, feeling all eyes on me. The schedule in my hands shakes as I look at my first period and back at him talking over the phone. He ends the conversation with an "Okay, thank you so much, goodbye," and walks over to me.

"They did not put you on the schedule. We apologize. They told me you are new, correct?" he says as he glances at the class. I nod my head and try to force a smile. "Why not introduce yourself?" he asks, smiling at the class.

I follow his lead, but my heart is going wild. I shake and try not to make a bad impression.

"Hello," I start with a slight crack in my voice as the class snickers. He snaps his fingers and points to me, signaling that the class should not behave negatively. My breathing is shortened, and I try to contain myself from crying, running out of the classroom, and then jumping off a bridge. All eyes are stuck on me, almost looking right through me, like fresh, pierced ears. I continue my introduction, wanting to get it over with and wanting those eyes off of me. "My name is Londyn McKay Scarlet, and I just moved from North Carolina."

I did not know what else to say. What does this teacher expect me to say? The teacher claps his hands in the quiet and awkward classroom. I can hear murmurs and whispers in some corners of the room while some are filled with small clapping noises. It soon stops as I simply stand here, still like a brick.

"You can take a seat right there," the teacher says, pointing beside a roly-poly young boy with curly, dirty blonde hair who was clearly sneaking his phone.

The teacher gets onto the kid, and I rustle between aisles to get to my destination. All eyes are still on me. 'Stop,' I want to yell. 'Stop looking at me, just stop!' I demand in my head. No one can listen to my thoughts, though. I am so thankful for this. I finally get into my seat, and the kid glances at me. Fortunately, the teacher claps to call everyone's attention to the front now that I am seated.

"Hello, class. I am Mr. William, your math teacher for the following semesters. I am thrilled to be teaching you all," he says as his voice echoes across the room, ringing my ears and making me jump every time he speaks. His voice quiets and silences as I focus on the posters and off-white walls in the classroom. Eventually, his voice becomes white noise as I take in my surroundings. I notice my desk wobbling every time I shift in my seat. I also notice that the floors have a certain pattern. "—Layla, are you paying any attention?"

My senses come back to me as I snap into focus. My head turns to the teacher as fast as a bullet. He is staring straight at me, having dubbed me Layla. I quickly open my mouth to answer him.

"Yes sir, and—" Oh no, I do not want to sound rude! "It's Londyn, sir."

He glances at me questionably, raises one eyebrow, and responds, "Right, pay more attention." Without waiting for me to reply, he continues to ramble and talk a mile a minute. My heart races from that incident, and I try to focus, not wanting to be caught unaware again.

The whole class period is just him chattering about what he likes. He only asks questions about three or four times to the class to "get to know them" or whatever. The bell rings, and everyone jumps from their seats, groaning. I do not blame them at all. Once most of the room clears out, I enter the hallway and look down at my schedule. Next up: S.T.E.M. I always wanted to be in S.T.E.M. It sounded interesting and exciting. My focus then shifts to where I am headed and the room number, which I will forget by the end of the school year.

I almost freeze at my thoughts. Why am I saying this? Why am I talking about the whole school year? Aren't my parents going to heal? Oh no… I do not want to think about that. I do not want to think about my mom being unhealthy. But wasn't she always unhealthy? She had a failing heart. I do not want to think about the possibility of her dying. I try to shake it out of my head. 'Quit it. Stop it. No more!' I say in my head, hot tears forming in my eyes and making my eyes sting. But what if she is dead right now, and I come home with the news that she passed? I think with more salty and hot tears bubbling in my eyes.

It is like I am blind now, as I cannot see a thing. All I can see is a blurry hallway filled with people, and I cannot hear anything but my racing thoughts. I clench my backpack tight as I pick up my pace, knowing the tardy bell will ring soon. I wipe my ugly tears and feel disgusting sweat under my armpits and on my head forming. The stress of everything constantly has me sweating. I eventually make it in the class as the students line up against a wall. I do my best to look like I was not crying a minute ago. I would just seem like a crybaby. I would seem like a pathetic lost puppy or something wanting to cling their energy onto somebody. It is a relief to me when the teacher starts talking.

"Hello, class! I am Mrs. Sullivan, your S.T.E.M. teacher for this semester. I am so glad to have you all!" She says enthusiastically. Does she not know everyone here does not want to be here at all? She appears to notice and clears her throat, holding herself a bit seriously. "I will order you accordingly. I will order you all by alphabetical order," she informs us, jogging to her desk and picking up her attendance sheet.

She begins to call out the last names of students. As each student steps forward, she points out where to sit and who to sit by. To my relief, my name is included this time, and I am called up next to sit beside a young Mexican girl with extremely long black hair tinted with a few unnatural colors. I sit beside her and patiently wait for the teacher to get finished. Since I want to get along, I decide to attempt a conversation with my seatmate.

"Hi," I say with an awkward smile, looking at her.

"Hello," she responds somewhat dryly.

Wow, leave it up to me to create awkward tension. I know I cannot let the conversation falter now, or it will haunt me for the rest of the day.

"I love your hair. I like the color magenta," I mention, trying not to trip over my words.

"Thank you," she says, flipping back some hair over her shoulder. I seem to have gotten her attention because she continues the conversation. "I did not see you last year. Are you new?" she asks, sounding puzzled.

"Yeah, I just moved here," I reply, smiling, as the tension is no longer awkward and uncomfortable.

"What is your name? Sorry, I know she just called out names, but I want to know your full name," She inquires with a smile and raised eyebrows.

"Londyn Scarlet," I introduce.

She looks impressed and has a wide and warm smile on her beautiful face. I find myself relaxing at her expression.

"That is one lovely name. I am Adriana Sanchez," She responds, still beaming at me.

"Thank you, and I love your name, too." I make sure she knows.

"Thank you." She smiles and says as she turns to give the teacher her full respect and focus.

"Alright, everyone, are you guys settled?" Mrs. Sullivan asks as she puts her paperback on her desk marked. Staring at Mrs. Sullivan as she speaks, I realize I never got a good look at her features when I first came into the classroom. She is lovely, her dark skin radiant under the classroom lights. Her outfit, jeans and a Tennessee sweatshirt, is casual but suits her well. Her hair, black, silky, and straight, is up. I notice she has a little scar or birthmark across her arm. That does not take away from her beauty. I focus my attention on her words, not wanting to miss anything, and embarrass myself by having to ask for help on the first day. "I want you all to fill out this 'All About Me' paper I am about to pass out right now. Work on this until the end of class, and when you do so, turn it into the yellow basket in the back. If you do not, work on it for homework."

Mrs. Sullivan starts passing out the papers. I, along with Adriana, am among the first to get one, and I look down at it. The paper poses simple questions, such as "What's your favorite color?" "Do you have any pets? If not, what would you want?" or "How old are you?" Some of these are not too hard to answer, so I try to fill in as many blanks as quickly as possible.

It is ridiculously hard to pick my favorite color. I look at Adriana's hair and then back at my paper, responding with, "Magenta." I do not have any pets. I am thirteen. Ah! The date and my name... I quickly jot down my name and date, messing up a few times. I did not know how much I deeply missed these projects until now. However, I start to think about the future projects I might have, and I groan under my breath. Pushing the thoughts back, I go back to writing my answers. I contemplate some answers since it is hard to answer what I want to be when I grow up. I still remember wanting to be a teacher when I was younger—but not anymore. 'This answer keeps coming up in my life... is it a sign?' I ponder to myself, shaking my head. Such silly thoughts. Of course, it is not a sign. It is quite a simple and frequent question to have and tell. Around me, students chatter and laugh in the background of my decision-making. I do not notice the time once again—like I know whenever we will leave anyway—and the bell rings, bringing the end to another class.

"Alright, class, have a good day and make smart choices!" Mrs. Sullivan hollers as we waddle our way out into the long hallways.

The day passes by, and soon, it hits the fourth period. The students head to lunch in a single file line, and I notice, upon stepping inside, that the lunchroom is crowded. I can hear laughter, snickering, and chattering across the room. It is the usual lunchroom soundtrack, not different from my last school. I pick up my tray and pick out the food that looks appetizing. I then pick out my juice and milk and wait in line again. Once it is my turn at the register, I look down at my card, which has my student number. I copy the numbers and punch them in.

"Have a great day," says the lunch lady with heavy eyelids and a forced smile.

I try to force a smile back, but when I step a bit further, I stop at once in my tracks. My smile turns into a frown as I scan the lunchroom and full seats. 'Where do I sit?' I ask myself. I look all over the lunchroom, finding an empty place, and sit one seat across from a girl. She looks a bit like me. I do my best not to stare, but she looks like me. I look away and down at my food to not make myself look like some creep. I quietly eat my food but soon notice the iconic magenta tints in someone's hair in my peripheral. It is Adriana.

"Hey, Londyn." She says, finally noticing me as I notice her.

"Hello," I answer with a smile. I blink as she gestures to the girl across from me and introduces her.

"This is my friend, Lainey."

Adriana's words ring through my ears. My breath catches, and my world tilts on its axis. No, it is just a coincidence, right? Ah! It must be. It cannot be her. Slowly, I turn my gaze to Lainey. The first thing I notice are her piercing blue eyes and dirty blonde hair with a seasick green tint in her hair at the end. She looks like me too much, not like twins, but like sisters, like half-sisters. I struggle to breathe, feeling relieved Lainey does not seem to have any qualms about filling the air.

"Hey—oh, my goodness, I love your shirt. I love the color navy blue!" she exclaims with a smile.

"Thank you," I respond, weakly chuckling at her compliment as I silently compose myself.

"I cannot explain navy blue. When you look at it, it feels like you are looking into a thousand stars," Lainey continues excitedly.

I nod and comment, "It does. It is a pretty color," with a smile creeping on my face. Much to my intrigue, we continue to chatter about our interests. I am comfortable. In fact, I scoot the seat next to me to be closer to them. I have a new friend, and I feel excited, but… I just cannot stop thinking about that journal. I am both relieved and saddened when lunch ends. Parting ways with Adriana and Lainey, I tell them I would see them later. The rest of the school day seems to fly by.

A few hours later, I am finally home. I do not have the

energy to inquire about everyone's day, but I make some conversation before informing everyone I have things to do. Soon enough, I begin my homework. I know it's the first day, and there is homework already. Earlier, I was told it was going to get worse. I sit at the bar and on the stool with my sheet of 'All About Me' from S.T.E.M. class. I answer all the questions until I am at the last one. It is unlike any other question. This one bothers me and makes me question myself…

The question: What makes you special?

Chapter Six

IT IS ONLY OUR FIRST TIME AT LIFE

Cookeville, Tennessee, August 11, 2018

A month has felt like years without my parents and being in my familiar space. Leaving home had been hard, but settling into a new place has been harder… It is Saturday. In the den, I am on my phone, aimlessly scrolling, but my mind is not focused on what's showing on the screen. My thoughts are cloudy as I continue to obsess over Papa's journal! It still feels surreal to have discovered these things about Papa, and my feelings toward him only grow colder and angrier. Everyone keeps looking at me, but they probably think I am still adjusting. How could I tell them I am reeling from Papa's betrayal and deceit? I shut off my phone since I cannot concentrate and advance towards my door as I hear someone speaking. I slightly open the door and realize it is Grandma calling out from the kitchen.

"Lon, dear?"

I do not know why she is calling me, and I quickly try to think if there is something I am supposed to be doing. Nothing comes to mind, so I let myself recall everyone's location in the house, wondering if we're supposed to be spending time together. That is not possible since I am sure everyone is doing something different. Avery is in our room while Ethan and Grandpa are out grocery shopping. I know Avery has headphones in since she is supposed to do homework. She always says she studies or works best when she has them. With no chores or family plans coming to mind, I breathe deeply and respond.

"Yes?" I ask, hoping I do not sound nervous or suspicious.

"Something the matter?" She asks me back.

Oh no. Why would Grandma ask me that? Does she realize my distance has been about something else? I immediately start praying in my head. I never mean to swear when I say, "Oh, Lord," I mean it—I am praying. What do I do? I cannot just straight up tell her I stole my Papa's journal and read half of it and went into a depressive episode where I read it and scrolled continuously on my phone while locking myself away, right? I feel hot tears forming in my eyes, and soon those tears spill over as the first tear goes down my cheek and onto my lips. I can taste it, reminding me of the taste of the salty ocean. I slowly close the door, backing into the den—but the thoughts that pop into my head race around, and suddenly, I do not want to be alone. Bursting out of my room, I run into the kitchen towards Grandma, hugging her like a small child.

"I am so sorry!" I exclaim loudly but quietly, not wanting to disturb Avery.

"Why are you sorry?" Grandma asks as she rubs my head and hugs me back.

Oh no, here it goes. It is on the edge of my throat, lingering and yearning to come out. Here it goes. I try to hold it in between sobs. Then it all comes out.

"Grandma, I stole Papa's journal! He is evil!" I shout. I no longer care who listens anymore, needing to get these feelings out. "He is evil! Pure evil!" I shout as I ugly cry.

I hear Avery stomping out of our shared room with a moue. Her scowling expression turns into a look of concern as she runs towards us.

"Londyn, Granny, what happened?" She asks.

I look at Avery with a lost expression and say, "It is Papa."

"Did he get well?" Avery asks. She reads our expressions again and looks as if she is at a loss for hope. "No?" she asks, her tone confused.

"Did you know he had a journal?" I ask her back. My heart pumps a mile a minute, and I hold a frown.

"It would be silly of him to," She responds, "What man carries a journal?"

"He did not carry one." I snap. "He hid it— he hid it from us."

I hate that man. I hate him so much. He hid everything away like it was nothing when it was tearing us all apart. He hid away his true feelings and let them fester, tearing us and Mama apart. How could he do this?!

"Show me," Avery demands as Grandma lets me go.

I storm off into our room, returning with a thick journal filled with dates and a lock. I pull out the key to unlock it.

"You hid it from us, too! You are no better!" Avery says, now realizing. Her face of concern turns into anger and disgust.

"No! I did not mean it like that!" I shout as Avery crosses her arms with furious eyebrows, body language screaming offense.

"I did not want you to worry about it like I was!" I retort, trying to back up my claim, knowing it sounds like those cheesy essay prompts. "I didn't want it to hurt you like it hurt me!"

"You could have just told us, and we could figure it out together... Isn't that what family is for, Londyn?" Avery asks, voice shifting into a sorrowful tone.

She's right... Now, I look and feel like a clown as the realization hits me. I did not have to suffer through this alone. I am so foolish. I want to bang my head on the kitchen counter a thousand times until I pass out. I want to run or go back in time and change all of this. My heart pounds violently and booms in my ears as I look at both Grandma and Avery. Grandma then takes my hand. She glances over to Avery and then me before she speaks.

"You are okay. We know now."

Those few words ring through my ears, soothing me. I know it sounds weird, but I almost sob at the relief they bring. Taking a deep breath, I then open the book to the page where it all started, where everything started. Every word of that note is invading my thoughts. I turn the journal to them as they read word for word. I am silent, waiting for their reactions.

"Sick monster," Avery murmurs.

It is a little funny to me because I know she knows Grandma is beside her and she cannot swear. If she did, she would get scolded—even in this situation. I stifle my slight amusement as I flip through the pages I read and show them. There is nothing dirty, as I reviewed some with them after moving to their side of the counter. Page after page, entry after entry, filled with his secrets. He wrote of his regrets about the life he had chosen. If it had only been one page of regret, maybe we could have seen past it... but everything shows his unhappiness with us, with Mama. It is too much to take, so I choose not to read anymore while Avery and Grandma continue on.

With them silently and intently reading, I space out and go to a different train of thought. I have not noticed any messages from Hailee. I never got Nolan's number. I always get butterflies thinking of him! But it is not the same without him around. I want to say the thought of him comforts me during these times. Though, I do think of good things that happened as well. I do have Lainey's number. I got it on Friday. I never knew it could be that easy. My life has been a mixed bag the last couple of months.

Noises from beside me break me out of my thoughts.

I watch as Avery grimaces and Grandma sits with a horrified look with wide eyes. Everything is coming out, and I cannot help but feel relief that I am no longer the only one who knows. As I process this, I hear the home telephone ring and hurry to answer it.

"Hello?" I greet—only to be left in shock! I pull the telephone away from me a bit and shout in a whisper, "It is the hospital!"

My announcement stuns Grandma and Avery. Handing the phone to Grandma, I wait beside Avery, us lingering for an answer. This has to be good news, right?! Finally, something good to come out of this mess! I am so excited, and I can tell Avery is excited, too. We wait for what feels like a thousand years, watching Grandma closely. However, I suspect we will not receive good news as Grandma's smile morphs into a frown as fast as lightning. She nods absently and says goodbye, hanging up the phone. She puts the phone back on the stand and looks at us with sorrow. Our excitement fades away at this.

"What did they say?" Avery asks as she stands up straight.

The only answer she receives is Grandma beginning to bawl uncontrollably.

"Grandma!" I say as she supports herself with the counter. My stomach feels like someone filled it with lead as Grandma cries and cries without ceasing. "G-Grandma, wha—"

"She is dead!" Grandma hollers. If she yells any louder,

I fear the house will shake loose from its foundation, filling with cracks like her voice.

"No— what?" I say in disbelief.

No, she cannot have said that. I must have heard her wrong. Mama could not be gone. I wrap my arms around myself, staring unseeingly. Mama cannot be gone… We hear the door open and close as the guys come inside, placing several groceries on the counter beside us. At the sight and sound of Grandma, the guys dash around the counter to see what is going on, Ethan leading the way.

"Hey now, what happened?" Ethan says.

His words only pierce my ears as I stand there with my mouth open and my eyes wide. I did not want to accept this. Everything sounds muffled, and I am unsure if it is Grandma or Avery who tells Ethan and Grandpa that Mama is gone. I do not know how to form words. Ethan looks like he wants to protest or shout in disbelief, but he stays silent. When his eyes fall on the journal, which is open to the first note that traumatized me, I can see his eyes looking over the words and processing the handwriting.

"What is this?" Grandpa asks weakly, glancing over Ethan's shoulder as he is visibly reeling from the news about Mama. "... Explain," he insists, obviously reading the words now.

"This is not a sick prank, right?" Ethan exclaims after a few seconds of silence.

"No, it is not," I finally speak, pushing away thoughts of Mama for a moment to remember my rage. Shaking my head, after opening and closing my mouth twice, I again let out my feelings. "Papa is evil."

I can see my declaration shakes Grandpa, but I cannot stop. All of the pain swells up inside of me. From Papa's betrayal to Mama's absence, I need to be heard.

"He is a sick man." I firmly state, "He is untrustworthy and not loyal to his family."

I gesture to the journal, urging them to read the note. They needed to see it in its entirety. None of us speak as they read it. After Ethan finishes reading the first note, he closes the journal before suddenly throwing it to the ground and covering his face. I wince as Ethan rubs his temples. Everything is overwhelming, but now we are all on the same page. I wish I could feel calm and relief, but all my emotions are brimming and overflowing inside me.

I watch Grandpa shake his head and walk outside to have a smoke break, trying to cope with all of this. I do not support the idea of smoking or the act of such, but right now, I understand. These emotions are too much to handle, and I feel the need to be alone. So, as I am about to stomp off to my room and crumble like a paper ball, Avery stops me. She pulls me into a hug, which Grandma joins in. Before I know it, Ethan also makes his way over to us... This is the final piece we need as we all break. Everyone starts to sob.

"We will be okay," Grandma says over our sobs. "You guys will grow old knowing your Ma was a good person, okay?"

We shake our heads in agreement and sniffle a bit,

quieting down. It is hard to come to terms with Mama being gone. The last time we saw her felt like goodbye. But it is hard to say goodbye. However, Grandma is right. Mama was a good, wonderful person. Once we feel stable enough, we all release each other. Before anyone can speak, the ringing of the phone breaks the silence. The sound makes me tremble, but there is no worse news we could receive than what we already have. Grandma answers the phone. Grandpa comes back inside, looking as tired as ever. His entrance is not nearly as noteworthy as Grandma's sudden anger. For Avery, Ethan, and me, this is the first time we have heard Grandma scream in rage. We know for sure she is upset when she gets all Southern-like.

"There is no way I'm letting you get these children, you murderer!" She hollers as her hand, which held the phone, shook in fear and rage.

We hear Papa yelling over the phone, "Give me my children, you hag!" But we do not get to hear more as Grandma shoos us away to go somewhere else rather than listening to their horrid argument.

We go off into our rooms, all lost in thought. Avery sits on her bed while I stand and look around distractedly. In all the time I've visited before, I never got to analyze the room well. Since we moved in, I had been preoccupied with other thoughts and hadn't really taken anything in. As I recall, this was my Mama's sister's room. Mama had three sisters. Four sisters altogether in one house? It sounds almost insane to me! That would be terrible for the parents having to deal with it, but my grandparents loved them anyway. Thinking of this, I am hit with emotions… I miss Mama. That sounds so childish, but right now, in my situation, I do. Shifting my thoughts back to the room to keep from crying again, I look at the sad, dead yellow walls. I know yellow is supposed to be a happy room, but it does not fit my current mood. The carpet is stained with a bit of lipstick and makeup. The traditional white doors are a little dingy. This place is now supposed to be home. I thank the Lord every day now that Avery and I have the same aesthetic and liking. If we did not, I know it would be chaos.

Finally, I move from my spot in the middle of the room and climb onto my bed. With the emotions that I have experienced today, I am beyond exhausted. I roll onto my side, able to hear Avery in her bed and close my eyes. I let my mind drift to other nonsensical things, hoping to find some peace. Amid my thoughts, I eventually fall asleep.

When I wake up, I see a notification for a missed call. I yawn, rub my eyes, and stare at the notification. It was Lainey. I am a little surprised to see she called me. With everything going on, I could use the distraction, so I decide to call her back. The phone rings for a moment until she picks it up.

"Hello?" She greets me, giving me room to respond.

"Hey, I saw that you called me," I say, still rubbing my eyes. I look over at Avery, who seems to be watching reels on her phone while letting the covers devour her.

"Oh, yes!" Lainey exclaims, "I was going to ask if

you wanted to spend some time at my house. Until the streetlights come on. Adriana will not be here since she has an appointment."

Despite my inner turmoil, I cannot help but get excited, knowing I could spend some time with her. Making a friend has given me something to hold onto these past few days. However, I feel like I am pushing Hailee away—and she must feel it, too, as she has not reached out. I do not want to see us drift apart, but I am at a loss of how to deal with it since I am away… Instead of dwelling on my relationship with Hailee, I refocus on Lainey and give her my answer.

"Yes! I would love to, but I must ask my grandparents first."

Muting myself, I go to my grandparents. It has been a few hours since I last saw them, but they look okay when my eyes land on them. They are on the couch with Grandma knitting a unique project and Grandpa sitting lazily and watching television. I wait a second before I clear my throat, gaining their attention.

"Hey, can I go to Lainey's house? It is just down the road," I request, hoping for permission. My grandparents look at me and nod with a smile. Grandma had seen her before, and Grandpa saw a glimpse of her one time. "I will be back when the streetlights come on," I reassure before I dash into the bedroom to get my bag.

I unmute myself and let Lainey know I can come over, and we hang up. I put everything that I needed in it. I pause for a moment as I wonder if I have forgotten something. I hear a slight snore from Avery, not realizing she had fallen asleep. I guess she had been dozing while looking at reels. My heart aches as I look at her. I hope she is all right. I also hope Ethan is, too. My eyes slowly fall on the journal on my bed. I do not remember bringing it into the room with me. 'Grandma must have done it while I was sleeping,' I think, recalling how Ethan had thrown it to the floor.

As I stare at the journal, I think suddenly of Lainey. My stomach knots and twists at the idea of telling her. I already know her last name: Mackenzie. I know it is her... I feel it is better to tell her right now. I had learned my lesson to not carry on this horrible secret for long. I know I will explode if I try to hold it in. Nodding, I put the journal in my bag, sling the bag over my shoulder, and take my phone. I walk out of the room and close the door quietly so as to not awaken Avery. While heading down the hallway, an idea pops into my head. I walk into the living room, staring at my grandparents, who look sad. Now, instead of watching TV, my grandpa is looking at a family picture with all four girls.

"Hey, afterward, can we burn this book? Did you not say we had a fire pit?" I question, grabbing their attention. "I think burning it could be good for all of us," I mumble.

"Yes, please," Grandpa responds, with Grandma nodding.

I nod along with Grandma, giving them both a small smile before heading out the door into the street, glimpsing the sunset. I walk along the sidewalk, wishing I had my bike with me. Walking is all right, but it just is not the same without my bike. As I think of my bike, I think of the last time I rode it. I start to get butterflies again, thinking of Nolan! I smile to myself, chuckling with my cheeks burning. Riding my bike had led me to Nolan, and even though it had been brief, I find myself thinking of him back in North Carolina.

However, as I think of home, I soon start thinking of my Mama, and my mood plummets as I consider everything that has led me to my mission and question involving Lainey. I sigh to myself, trying to grasp these thoughts and feelings whirling around inside me. Keeping my eyes peeled, I search for the house number Lainey gave me and eventually find her house. My heart beats a little faster as I make my way up to the door. Shakily, I knock on the door, and my heart skips a beat as I wonder if I am making the right choice. A beautiful woman answers the door before I can reconsider and back out, leaving me awestruck. I take in her blue eyes and bouncy, short, curled blonde hair. She has a slim figure and is distractingly tall.

"You must be Londyn?" She questions, pulling me out of my daze.

"Yes, ma'am," I say, trying to have good manners.

"Come inside," she invites, stepping back to let me in. "You girls have fun. I'll be in the living room if you girls need me."

I must admit it is a delightful home. It is spacious and big. I walk inside and take my shoes off, setting them neatly with the other shoes surrounding the entryway. I move in further, looking around, and my view soon fills with Lainey. I grin, and she grins before leading me to her bedroom.

"Hi!" She greets enthusiastically, spreading her arms out with a small 'Tada!' motion. "Here is my bedroom, I guess," she says, putting her arms down and closing the door behind her.

Her room is very colorful, with fairy lights hanging from the ceiling and LED lights around the wall trim. Drawings and posters are all over the walls. Her bed is positioned off to the side, with a blue comforter on it and lots and lots of pillows. Her room is comfortable and cozy, and I can relax. I already know how much I enjoy Lainey's company, so we have lots of fun without my awkwardness mucking up the space.

However, it still does not fully distract me from the fact that Mama is gone, and Papa is a cheater and murderer. I and everyone else believe he drove that car into that building on purpose. I say he got mad, argued with Mama, and decided to end things on his terms. The journal spoke of his unhappiness and lack of love for Mama. There is nothing else to explain how the car crashed into the side of the building. As I sit, thinking over how to bring the subject up, I jolt out of my thoughts as I hear Mrs. Mackenzie yelling at someone over the phone. With everything I know and believe, I am sure I know who it is. But Lainey does not.

We listen patiently. I can make out certain comments like, "No, I am not interested in it!" and "No, I said no!"

along with, "You are not coming here, and you aren't welcome either!" Soon enough, Mrs. Mackenzie slams something like a drawer, and the talk is muffled. For a moment, it is awkward as silence fills the air. I look over at Lainey, wondering what she is thinking. She clearly feels the weight of my gaze and starts to talk.

"I normally hear her talk to a man… Though, she sometimes alternates between flirting or hollering," Lainey admits, looking at the ground and then at her freshly painted nails—which had been one of our fun activities.

My heart beats fast as I want to tell her so badly about all this history! It is not fair for her to be left in the dark. I know how that feels now. So, mustering up my courage, I open my mouth.

"Lain, pinky promise me you will not tell anyone else. This is between you, me, and my family, okay?" I say, holding out my right pinky as she gets all wide-eyed. She hooks her pinky with mine, and we hold them briefly before releasing them. I pull out the journal from my backpack and unlock it. "I think the man is my Papa," I reveal, scooting the book towards her.

"That is silly," she responds, scoffing in disbelief. I understand her initial reaction, so I do not get offended. I watch as she flips to the page that I yearn for her to read. Soon, things change… Her small smirk turns into a frown before morphing into horror the more she reads. She shakes her head. "No, it cannot be! It just cannot be! I know I have a stepdad, but…"

I can see everything is starting to make sense for her.

She stares at me, and I cannot help but frown, looking back at her. My friend, my half-sister, is trying her best to process this truth. I only hope I have not hurt her with this knowledge. Closing the journal and tossing it back into my bag, I zip my bag up and turn my attention back to her, wanting to reach out and hug her.

"Are you okay?" I ask with concern.

"Yeah, knowing I have an actual sister!" She answers.

"Well, two half-sisters and one half-brother." I correct her, watching her eyes get wide.

"Right!" she exclaims.

I am relieved that she seems accepting of everything. As I look behind her and see the streetlight lit up, I know it is time for me to go. So, I begin collecting my things and trying to gather my thoughts. I meant it when I told her that this is a secret between us and my family. I make sure to let her know how serious I am as I tell her the fate of the journal.

"I am going to burn this journal, and that will be it," I inform her once I put my bag over my shoulder.

She doesn't react outwardly to my words, but I feel sure she understands why. I get up, and so does she. Before I know it, she is hugging me tightly. I hug her back, feeling some tension ooze out of me. Releasing her, I step back and offer a small smile.

"I will see you at school," she says as I leave her bedroom.

"See you!" I speak.

I take one more peek at her before I leave. She looks

sad. I do not blame her. It feels really messed up telling someone something so life-changing and then leaving, but I did not want to get in trouble—plus, I want to burn this journal for good as soon as possible. Hopefully, we will get to talk more and clear the air further. Mrs. Mackenzie sees me from the living room and waves goodbye as I leave. I wave back, wondering if she will ever tell Lainey everything she knows. It is not my business, but I cannot help but wonder…

Outside, I breathe in the fresh air and start going home. It is not nighttime yet, so I am still in the clear. I check my phone and read 5:46 P.M. There is plenty of daylight left for what needs to be done, but I find myself picking up my pace and hurrying back. I am a little out of breath when I arrive. I knock on the door to the house, and Avery answers it with a smile. I walk inside and close the door behind me, Avery wandering ahead. Everyone is in the kitchen or living room. We had told each other over the summer that we would try to spend time with each other and not be a hermit. So, I quickly open up to propose the family activity for the day.

"Who is ready to burn a journal?"

"Me!" Ethan answers, jumping up and raising his hand. This is the first time in quite a while that I have seen him smile, and I cannot help but smile back.

"Alrighty, let us go!" Grandma says, wiping tears from her face and heading to the back door to the backyard.

Once we're all outside together, we collect sticks and throw them in the fire pit. Starting the fire, we watch the flames flicker and dance. When there is enough heat, I do not hesitate to throw the journal in the fire. I do not have a second or opposing thought to my action. Gathered together, we watch the fire grow bigger, with the journal feeding it.

I watch the reason for all of this go into flames—literally. I watch it turn into ash and nothing more. I watch that journal die. I see every flame biting into the journal and devouring it. It feels good watching it die away. I know I will keep these memories and traumatic events with me, but the words of the journal are no longer.

Now, I understand that asking for help during a challenging time is not so bad. I understand now. Now I understand everyone has a secret; sometimes, secrets can take away other people's happiness. My life is not the way it once was. There are no more trips to the coffee shop and watching Coraline through the window. There are no more sleepovers with Hailee, where we build forts and stay until our eyes feel heavy. There are no more bike rides, which led to me crashing into Nolan. I know I will never see Nolan again.

It is crazy how strongly I feel for Nolan at this moment. I just want him to hold me and tell me everything he likes. I want him to talk to me again, revealing things about himself that no one else knows. I am now the new kid, and I can empathize with how he feels being in a new place. Everything is going to remind me of him for a time. But that is okay because it will remind me how to let go. Mama's passing hurts like nothing I have ever felt, but

I remember her sweet smile and gentle words. I know I have to move past this moment in my life. This time will remind me how life will move on. And so, I will too…

So should you, dear reader.
But perhaps,
And just maybe,
Things are not supposed to stay in our lives forever,
Including people,
They will pass by quickly like the seasons,
cycling through the blossoming Spring, the sweltering Summer,
the withering Fall, and the chilly Winter,
But secrets are the ghost that haunts us,
They follow us to our graves,
They will lay by our skeletons until we let go.
Sometimes, you cannot just let go of such things. I know it is difficult. Just trust in time, and soon, you will see. You will understand, just as I do. Not fully, but a good bit.
Do not fret. It is only our first time at life.

ACKNOWLEDGMENTS

I would like to thank my publisher for giving me the opportunity to publish this book and helping me throughout this incredible journey. I would also like to thank my family, friends, and teachers for giving me great support. Special thanks to my editor, Terrica Singletary. I acknowledge that I have worked tremendously hard on this novella. Lastly, I would like to thank you, dear reader, for accepting and recognizing this book. Thank you, once again.

Sincerely,
Addison Mott

CONNECT WITH THE AUTHOR

The Young Authors Initiative (YAI) is a Keen Vision Publishing, LLC (KVP) program designed to help young writers, specifically in middle school, achieve their goal of becoming a published author.

ADDISON MOTT is of the 2024 YAI group. She is a storyteller who enjoys writing stories that people can relate to. For more information about Addison and the YAI program, visit **www.publishwithkvp.com**